A SHORT HISTORY OF FLORENCE
FRANCO CARDINI

Pacini
Collection

From the origins to 1860

2

© Copyright 1999 by Pacini Editore S.p.A.

First published 1999
Reprinted 2003, 2006

English translation by Amanda Mazzinghi

ISBN 88-7781-493-4

Photocopies may be made for the reader's personal use, on the condition that they do not exceed 15% of the total volume and payment is made to SIAE in accordance with article 68, codicil 4 of the Law of 22 April 1941 no. 633, i.e. the agreement stipulated between SIAE, AIE, SNS and CNA, CONFARTIGIANATO, CASA, CLAAI, CONFCOMMERCIO, and CONFESERCENTI on 18 December 2000.
Permission from the Publisher/copyright holder must be obtained for the reproduction of this material for any other purpose than the one specified above.

CONTENTS

Preface .... pag. 5

A river, a bridge, a road .... » 8

Celestial patrons, earthly protectors,
surrounding walls .... » 19

A city of warriors and merchants .... » 28

The apogee .... » 47

Crisis and redefinition of a "bourgeois"
city .... » 69

A town for the prince .... » 89

Sons of Jove and of the rain of gold .... » 104

The age of the Lorraine family .... » 115

PREFACE

Florence belongs to that small group of cities whose history may be told too amply in a few lines or too sketchily in many volumes. A true history of Florence, a history concerned with the heart of the story – like the true history of Rome or Athens or Jerusalem – is in the end the history of our entire civilisation; the writer who looks into it deeply enough finds it so rich that even the fullest, most analytical account of it could not do it justice.

But for this very reason, perhaps, a "Short History" may be useful to many readers, from the student to the more focused type of tourist to the Florentine who would feel discouraged faced with a full treatment of the subject but who does not want to give up the search for a *vademecum*, which will help him draw from his experience, his memories, his sensations, and his feelings too, an all-inclusive image of a remarkable – a unique – city .

To call Florence remarkable and unique does not exempt one from the duty of reflecting on her history and attempting rational comment. What has made her what she is, over the centuries? How can she still be considered exceptional today? Is there real fascination there, apart from media hyp and the tourist industry? And her history, which someone called "splendid," hasn't it got another face?

A history book, however brief, has as its object a past, recent or distant, but it is written in and for the present. When an essay like this one has as its aim the "original characteristics" of a great artistic centre which is also a great twentieth-century city with its problems and its crises, it is even more urgent that the essay furnish answers that will limit the characteristics and historical assumptions of those problems and crises. And in a city like Florence, afflicted with confusion and decay which one can seek to explain but not deny, such a task is neither easy nor pleasant.

There is not a city in the world that does not feel, for good or ill, the weight of its past. But in Florence, and for Florence, this weight is on the one hand crushing, while on the other hand it is the thing that shapes the life of today. At the urban and monumental level, this tallies very obviously, even if perhaps with less dramaticity than in Venice (but much more than happens for many other historic centres). It is, all the same, the heritage of the past in terms of cultural and traditional significance that still conditions life, the nature of society, the policies, the tastes, the economy and the image of Florence and the Florentines. Here the past is not simply past: it is an integral part of the present, one lives it – indeed one relives it, one even "reinvents" it – as the present, one plays it over again as if it were indivisibly bound to the present. From the significance of Florence in the

Risorgimento – the "ballot boxes of the strong" in Santa Croce, the Arno in which they came to "dip their clothes" in that Italian language without which no plausible plan of uniting Italy could have been envisaged – to her most modern and recent political proposals, or the most "in" images of crafts and high quality fashion which still bring Florence to the attention of the world, there is no aspect of the life of the city or of the activities of her people which does not give the impression of being first and foremost a kind of paper currency which is valued because it is guaranteed by the gold reserves of the Florentine past. It is a past made of memory, a memory of the political past, as well as of art, churches and museums.

This is a city unlike any other, yet a universal city; a city in some ways enclosed – more than she seems – in a sort of lingering, grim provincialism of which she is at times downright proud; but at the same time a city that can truly claim to be the glory of the world. Between the thirteenth and nineteenth centuries she was well able to dominate, by various rights and in various ways, a "regional state", Tuscany; and when she became part of a broader, national unit, to whose cultural identity and justification she had contributed, she became for a short time the nation's capital. But she was born to be what she is, and this role was too restricting. Florence owes her role to the freedom and enterprise of the Florentines, to their capacity to look beyond the temporal limits of the present and the geographical limits of the peninsula. For this reason – without denying the importance of the prospects that opened up in the new Italy of 1860 – we have chosen to stop this "brief history" at the double loss of independence and dominion over the other Tuscan cities. If post-unification Florence meant something, indeed a great deal, to united Italy, it was owing to the memory of – and in some measure to the pride in and nostalgia for – the days of Florentine liberty and those of the Medici Princes. This profile of Florentine history sets out to present not so much the events and institutions of the city as a search for the characteristics that make up her identity.

A river, a bridge, a road

Cities, like people, bear traces – in their exterior aspect, in their urban structure, in that complex of tangible and intangible characteristics that makes their "atmosphere" – of their past: the glories, the inconsistencies, the sufferings, the mistakes. Even to the visitor who knows little of history Rome still speaks the language of her ancient splendours, of her medieval devastation punctuated by grim, warlike rocks and beautiful basilicas, her Renaissance and baroque vigour, her Umbertine pomp; she speaks of Fascist rhetoric in her neo-neo-classical pillars and arches and futuristic extravaganzas recycled in colossal dreams. Milan tells a hard but triumphant story of her years as a great Roman and Christian capital in the fourth and fifth centuries, and those in which she was ruled by a duke or by a *commune* and established her military or manufacturing strength; she speaks in the water of her canals within the city, by now mostly filled in but at one time pulsating with life and activity. She speaks of her love for the machines which already, during the years of the closed Viscounties, foreshadowed the industrial future, and finally of the enlightened Hapsburg despotism and the strenuous years of the Napoleonic dictatorship, both of them preludes to her establishment as a European metropolis. Palermo tells us stories of splendid and desolating happenings in her Arab and Norman memories, her "colonial" gardens, her Spanish baroque and her *art nouveau* buildings.

To anyone visiting Florence for the first time – or any time that felt like the first – with the help of a good, ordinary tourist map, the Roman imprint would seem to be clearly stamped on the city. At the same time, in the right-angled network of streets in the centre the visitor would see the desire to rationalise, which, between the nineteenth century and the early twentieth, tried to make the city "healthy" and "modern". In some of the street names (Via del Campidoglio (Capitol), Via delle Terme (thermal baths), Via di Capaccio (*Caput aquae*, headwaters, source) he would see the Roman plan of the city, which appears also in the curious structure of the buildings between Piazza Peruzzi and Piazza Santa Croce, which are curved because they were built on the foundations of the amphitheatre. But the visitor realises at once – from the forbidding towers built of massive stone, from the airy yet grim Renaissance palaces, from the churches, the most beautiful of which were built between the Romanesque and mannerist periods (though in many cases altered at various times) – that the city's great period, her "golden age" as they say, was between the third and the sixteenth centuries. It was such an exalted, glorious, significant age that the Florentines seem to have gone on dreaming about it long after it came to an end; so much so that the more astute tourist will have no difficulty in discerning, in the continual repetition of "medieval" and "renaissance" shapes and designs everywhere, an abundance of imitations, quotations and arbitrary, over-elaborate restoration. This is the neo-gothic and neo-renaissance look imposed on the city in the nineteenth and twentieth centuries, which is confused, but never fused, with the true Middle Ages and the real Renaissance which so enriched Florence. While these additions are striking, the visitor will be equally moved by what is lacking. At first sight, Florence will seem to him to be "a city devoid of the baroque". On closer examination it becomes clear that there is baroque to be found, and baroque of high quality, from the delicate architecture of San Gaetano to the sumptuous Santissima Annunziata. But this is a temperate baroque, closely linked to the mannerist tradition; it reminds one of the prose of Galileo Galilei, so dry, limpid and deliberately remote from the frills fashionable in his time; it is a baroque – later continued by the eighteenth century of physiocracy and the Enlightmenment – that is all realism and scientific spirit, which makes itself felt above all – one would say – in the brass of the scientific instruments in the Specola or the Science Museum, or in the austere old carved wooden shelves of the Laurentian and Marucellian libraries. This baroque and this eighteenth century reflect the sombre decline of the house of Medici and the serene, at first unscrupulous and later soporific, Hapsburg-Lorraine government.

But other discoveries, not all of them pleasant, will make the tourist more alert and the Florentine more observant, if they are prepared to cast an eye over the city without overlooking the clues as to what was once there and is there no more. Here and there, unequivocal signs of pomp, magniloquence, order – perhaps also hygiene and cleanliness, how much less in the intentions – recovered and imposed from outside, one does not know with how much respect for the history, the traditions and the truest needs of the city: as, for instance, in the nineteenth-century General Insurance building in Piazza Signoria, right opposite Palazzo Vecchio, with its frigid lines inspired by an imitation of an academic conception of the fifteenth-century; or in the vast Piazza Repubblica, which speaks the language of nineteenth-century clearances, which certainly did get rid of some frightful buildings but which also compromised the balance of history in the architectural styles of the city centre; or in girdle of boulevards linked by piazzas, echoing Promis's Turin and Haussmann's Paris with all the implications, political and ideological, of those decisions relived, however, more quietly, with less rhetoric and less functionality.

Yet it is still true that, if you take in Florence at a single glance, she still appears today – notwithstanding incongruities, violence and breakages, which there have certainly been – as if conceived in a wonderful unity and constructed all at one go. The Romanesque bulk of San Miniato, the sixteenth-century mass of San Salvatore and of the Fort of San Giorgio, and the nineteenth-century architecture of Piazzale Michelangelo somehow, mysteriously, live together in harmony; and on the city skyline, which you can admire from the balustrade of the Piazzale, no harm is done to the austere line of Ponte Vecchio and Giotto's bell tower and the bell tower of Santa Croce by the neo-classical Exchange or by Santa Maria Novella and

Michelucci's railway station, so different and so perfectly paired, or by the copper green of the beautiful Sephardic synagogue, or by the upward thrust - aggressively square – of the tower of the stadium.

Yet wounds there are, some old, some not so old. Wandering among the towers that have now been done up into flats, and the anonymous, fifties-style buildings in the Ponte Vecchio area always gives you a pang if you are one of those who still remember what that area between Piazza Pitti, Piazza Frescobaldi, the Santa Trinita bridge and the New Market (the "Porcellino" to non-Florentines) was like until the end of '44, or if you know what it was like from Alinari's photographs. A visit to the working-class areas of San Frediano and Santa Croce rouses one to angry protest; here the dreadful, insanitary houses of yesterday are being rapidly added to, or replaced, by the pseudo-antique and post-modernist rebuilding perpetrated by crooked dealers who are selling the city to the tourist industry and building speculators. And, to anyone who knows how to look at the walls, the many plaques with inscriptions relating to the floods – from the famous one of 1333 to the 1966 disaster still vivid in many memories – are reminders of wounds dealt to the city's heritage that have never been healed, and of problems glossed over rather than solved.

Ponte Vecchio; the father-master-stepfather Arno; the urban grid of Roman origin, which has survived and been constantly rediscovered. A bridge; a river; a road which, crossing this thanks to that, gave life to a narrow plain, cutting a furrow through it from south to north, towards the hills between Fiesole and Monte Morello. This is the scenery in which Florence was encamped – and still is. It may not be immediately obvious why the city prospered; the reasons are many and varied; but it is clear enough what made her take root where she did: a river, a bridge, a road.

The two ridges which run north and south of the Arno narrow, when they reach the mid-point of its course, to form two gorges through which it flows narrow and deep: Incisa to the east and Gonfolina to the west. Between these two points, the line of hills – Monte Albano to the west, Monte Giovi to the north, and to the south the hills which further down become the Chianti chain – broaden out into an amphitheatre until they form, on the right bank of the river, a fairly broad plain, roughly fifty metres above sea level. In the quarternarian era that plain was filled by a lake, one of the many which were scattered all over Tuscany until they were drained in the eighteenth-century; when the waters of the lake withdrew, they left the place a barren wasteland of stagnant pools and swamps. There are still traces of them, especially to the north-west, between Sesto, Campi Bisenzio and Signa; or to the south-east, in the area of Ripoli and the old "Bisarno", where a few place names recall the "blades", the strips of stagnant water where it was once easy to hunt, fish and catch malaria.

It is a plain of modest dimensions: about forty kilometres long (east-west) and more or less ten kilometres wide. These are the limits within which today's "greater Florence", necessarily oblong in shape, has developed. For a long time it was uninhabited territory, owing to the impossible environmental conditions. Between the tenth and the eighth centuries B.C. a modest settlement probably arose, where the centre of the city now is, and was later abandoned. Between the seventh and sixth centuries B.C. the Etruscans singled out, more or less in the middle of the area, a point at which the river could be forded with relative ease; however, they took care, as they always did, not to found a settlement in the plain. They picked out a hill about six kilometres from the ford and there founded the fortified city of Fiesole, surrounded by strong walls. It was firmly planted on the edge of the territory north of the Arno inhabited by Ligurians and Italics but crossed by the road connecting the Etrurian settlements, properly so called, with the Etruscan settlements of northern Italy, which had not yet been disrupted by Celtic expansion.

However, Florence, or rather Florentia, really was what the fourteenth-century memorialists wanted her to be: the daughter of Rome. Archaeologists continue to disagree about the pre-Roman settlement which, in one form or another, seems to have existed, and about the proto-Roman *municipium* at the confluence of the Arno and the Mugnone (the latter of which flowed more to the east then than it does today) which was destroyed by Silla because it was guilty of having supported the Marian party. What is certain is that the Arno ford began to acquire importance when the Via Cassia had to cross the river in order to connect Rome with Cisalpine Gaul. It is thought that the city arose in 59 B.C., just north of the Arno and east of the Mugnone, to dominate the confluence of the two rivers; and that its name, Florentia, is traceable to the *Floralia* festivals which were celebrated between the end of April and the first few days of May. The Roman engineers' method of planning the network of roads and the perimeters of the agricultural districts by dividing land into "hundreds" has marked the whole area indelibly: its unmistakable traces can still be seen on topographical maps and aerial photographs.

Roman Florence was a settlement modelled on the traditional shape of the military *castrum* (camp): a quadrangle surrounded by walls, about 1800 metres on each side, with 10,000 to 15,000 people living inside. The quadrangle was constructed on two main streets. The first was the *cardo maximus*, running north and south; it was more or less the part of the Via Cassia that crossed the city and was the continuation of the part which, coming from the south side of the Arno (nowadays known as the *oltrarno*), crossed the river by the bridge, first made of wood and then of masonry, later known as Ponte Vecchio. The second main street was the *decumanus*, which ran east and west. Four gates stood at the points where the two streets touched the surrounding walls. The *cardo maximus* followed more or less the course of the present-day Via Calimala and Via Roma; the *decumanus* that of Via del Corso, Via degli Speziali and Via Strozzi. Where the cardo maximus and the *decumanus* intersected each other, and where the Old Market stood in old Florence (before 1860) and later Piazza Vittorio Emanuele II which later still became Piazza della Repubbica, was the Campidoglio, the Capitol.

One or two reliable pieces of information about Florence begin to appear in the second century A.D., that is to say, when, in about 123, the New Cassia was opened, and the bridge replaced the ferry by which the river had up to then been crossed. By the end of that century the city was already provided – outside her walls – with a river port, an amphitheatre, an aqueduct from Monte Morello and thermal baths; and in 285, when Diocletian changed the hierarchy of the administrators working directly under the Emperor, the seat of the *Corrector* responsible for Tuscia (later called Tuscany) was established in Florence.

The economic prosperity of the city did not come solely from Cassia. From the first century A.D. it seems that it was conditioned by dealings with the Tyrrhenian port of Pisa, dealings which were due to the navigability of the Arno. The cult of Iside may have reached the city through oriental merchants, but from the Orient came the first Christian evangelisers too. It is true that the first great cult of the new religion, that attributed to the deacon Lorenzo, goes back to the days of the Roman city ; but the Palestinian saint, Felicity, and Miniato, or rather Mynias (an Armenian king in the later legend), came from the east. Miniato, Florence's first martyr, was beheaded in 250 during Decius's persecution. He is one of those saints, like the Parisian Dionigus, who pick up their heads and carry them. Miniato set off, carrying his head, towards the hill, on the south-east side of the city, which he had chosen beforehand for his burial. There the splendid basilica dedicated to his memory was later built.

These are legends, of course. But it is accepted as fact that Florence had her own bishop, Felix, from the time of Constantine; that she was visited by Ambrose who gave the young diocese prestige by a gift of relics and by contributing to the foundation of the basilica of San Lorenzo, just outside the city walls. It is also accepted that Florence found a first *pater patriae* (father of the homeland) in Bishop Zanobi (the Florentine version of another oriental name, Zenobius) who in 405 stirred up the Florentines to resist the Goth Radagaiso who had laid siege to the city and was then defeated and executed by Stilicone, the great general of the Emperor Honorius. Thanks to Zanobi, the entire citizenry of Florence thereupon embraced the new religion, abandoning whatever was left in it of paganism. The Syriac saint, Reparata, was in consequence chosen as patron of the city. It was on her day that Florence had been liberated from the threat of Radagaiso.

Celestial patrons, earthly protectors, surrounding walls

A long eclipse seems to envelop the history of Florence between the fifth and ninth centuries, like that of the other centres of the old Western-Roman world; almost all of them were involved in the long process of disintegration and convulsed by incessant "barbarian" raids. In the city's memories recorded by the chroniclers of the third and fourth centuries (or reconstructed by them) the city was destroyed by Attila; but the confused information that has come down to us from those distant centuries is evidently somewhat misleading. It was not the Hun who was responsible for the destruction of the city (which was in any case only partial) but the Ostrogoth Totila. Florence was involved in the war between the Greeks and the Goths. Subject, like most of Italy, to the rule of Theodoric, she was occupied by the Byzantines in 541, sacked and partially devastated by Totila in about 550, and later reconquered by the

Greeks. At that time the city was so shattered and depopulated that when the Byzantines tried to restore the defences they tightened the ring of city walls by tens of metres, on the north, east and west: what it came to was that the city was bounded on the south-west by the ruins of the baths, on the north-west by the Campidoglio, and on the south-east by the theatre (the area occupied today by Palazzo Vecchio).

And so, reduced to a heap of hovels and rubble (which nevertheless bore traces of a noble past), Florence, in about 570, fell into the hands of the Longobards, who left their imprint on her but gave greatest importance – in Tuscany – to Lucca. One of the chief problems of the Longobards was the difficulty of maintaining their position far enough from the Apennines, which were too close to the lines of the Byzantines, who controlled the Adriatic coasts of the peninsula and also the swampy Tyrrhenian coast.

The result of all this was the decay of the arterial roads such as the Via Cassia and the Via Aurelia and the development of a new route of communication between the Po plain and Rome crossing territory under the unchallenged dominion of the Longobards. This route (later known as the "Via Francigena") descended from Cisa, passed through Lucca and, braving the marshy area of the middle and lower Arno valley between Empoli and

Fucecchio, went on southward by means of the track through the Valdelsa.

It did not take in Florence and thus it condemned her to an isolation which was among the causes of her decline.

Yet the Longobard occupation remains more evident than one thinks. Like many other newly converted peoples, the Longobards were devoted to St. John the Baptist, and it is probably owing to them that he became the new patron saint of Florence, to some extent overshadowing Zanobi and Saints Lorenzo, Reparata, Miniato and Felicita, and recognised for a long time as the very symbol of the city. In the golden age of the Commune he was spoken of – and the legend was revived by Dante – as an ancient protector of Florence, the pagan Mars, whose statue stood for a long while on the highest point of his temple, to be later removed and placed on the bridgehead of Ponte Vecchio. Though later eroded and battered, it was probably, at the time, a good likeness of a barbarian chief, perhaps Totila himself, and people would have attributed to it a sort of arcane power over the city, an ambiguous power, half threatening and half protective. The ancient, crumbling protector watched over Florence, although she had repudiated him, and the city-state ran no risk while a vestige of his cult remained.

But, although it was of course dedicated to St. John the Baptist, the baptistery was identical with the legendary "temple of Mars". It was built in the eleventh and twelfth centuries (for a time it was even used as the cathedral), but it seems that it was erected on a fifth-century foundation. It was on that account true that the Florentine palladium, the "Beautiful St. John" (as Dante called it), was in some way connected with the Roman world, if not with the pagan heritage.

This was not the only legend that possessed a slightly distorted and obscured nucleus of truth. In 1553 the prior of the beautiful little Romanesque church of the Holy Apostles (SS. Apostoli), between the Arno and the remains of the ancient buildings of the thermal baths, put up a marble stone which, though its position has been changed, can still be read on the façade of his church. It tells how on 6 April 805, in the presence of Turpinus, Roland and Oliver, Charlemagne – falling back on Florence from Rome – had founded the church, which Archbishop Turpinus had consecrated in person. Another legend, even less clear in its constituent elements, appeared in the eighteenth and nineteenth centuries, concerning a horshoe of Charlemagne's or else of Roland's, or at the very least its imprint, on the door of the splendid church of Santo Stefano in Ponte, not far from SS. Apostoli. The memory of the names and deeds of Charlemagne and the paladins was strong in Florence, and in the fifteenth century Donato Acciaioli recast his life in fine humanistic Latin, not without clear political references to the French crown. Again it was the chroniclers of the thirteenth and fourteenth centuries who were responsible for the information that, in the early years of the ninth century, Charlemagne had refounded the city of Florence, razed to the ground by Attila and Totila and from that time never rebuilt, although many eminent families had continued to live on, at a short distance from the ruins of their city.

However, it seems that Charlemagne did come to Florence twice, or at least spent a short time in Florentine territory: first in 781, returning from Rome (and perhaps on that occasion he paid homage to the martyr Miniato, on the hill overlooking the little city); and then again in 786, when he received the complaints of certain monks about the Longobard duke Gudibrando.

These facts do not seem, on examination, to be in any way significant. Nothing indicates that they can be assumed as proof of some meritorious contribution of the great Frankish Emperor to the rebirth of Florence. If anything, the opposite is true: these seem to be episodes that have been arbitrarily attached to that rebirth at a later date. But the chronology, even if it has little claim to be taken seriously, has a certain objective force: it is a fact that Florence was reborn early in the ninth century, in spite of the menace of the Vikings who were attacking neighbouring Fiesole; and the rebirth of the West, in Charlemagne's time and after him, certainly has something broadly speaking to do with the rebirth of Florence.

More than to Charlemagne – who, however, did replace the Longobard duke with a Frankish count – it is to Lothario I that we owe several measures which helped the city's recovery: in 854 he put the two counties of Florence and Fiesole together under a single count, who lived not in the ancient Etruscan centre on the high ground but in the more recent Roman centre on the river bank. A few years later the western part of the diocese of Fiesole lost several parishes to Florence. Thus began a process which continued for a long time and led to Fiesole being swallowed by Florence.

By then, no other county* in Tuscany was as big as this. It shared a boundary with three others: Arezzo to the east, Pistoia to the west and Siena to the south. Meanwhile Florence expanded and its surrounding walls were strengthened. This was a good thing, though the cause was not: the Magyar raids of the first half of the tenth century probably contributed to the growth of the city, by leading people who lived too insecurely in the rest of the county to move into the city. A third circle of walls was now built, replacing the original Roman circle and the later, smaller, Byzantine one: it covered, more or less, the lines of the Roman walls and took in the residential districts which had

---

* The word county is used throughout this book in the sense of "the territory belonging to, or ruled by, a count".

grown up in the area south of the north side of the old quadrangle. Florence now looked as if she had grown by an area more or less corresponding to a sort of scalene triangle which, starting from the north gate (where the Via Cassia, leaving Ponte Vecchio, entered the city) had as vertices the area of the theatre and the present-day Piazza de' Giudici, until it reached the river port. Now, the walls ran parallel to the Arno and only a few metres from it.

At the end of the tenth century the Marquis Hugo of Tuscany, son of the great lady who had founded the Florentine *badia* (abbey), left Lucca to live in Florence. Not many years before, Emperor Henry II founded a beautiful church on the hill sacred to the burial of San Miniato, martyr. The church was faced with white marble from Carrara and green marble from Pisa, divided into geometric panels, with Corinthian capitals and a great central tympanum, characteristics displaying a love of the antique and of classical modules on which Florence was to base her highly original artistic idiom.

Round about the middle of the tenth century a lucky combination of circumstances catapulted her into the centre of the political and religious scene. The new Marquis of Tuscany, Geoffrey of Lorraine, chose Florence – in which a great council of reform had been held in 1055 – as his capital. Geoffrey's brother was Pope Stephen IX, a strong champion of moral reform among the clergy and a supporter of the

Imperial programme for that cause. And for a short time, from 1059 to 1061, a bishop of Florence, Gerardo, ascended the throne of St. Peter with the name of Nicholas II and performed his role as Pope without giving up that of Bishop of Florence. When, with the death of Emperor Henry III and the minority of his successor Henry IV, reformist circles within the Church considered the moment had come to do without the restraint exercised by the secular power in carrying out their programme, events in Florence seemed to them to offer a perfect example. The situation there had been developing since about 1035, when matters were set in train by a convert, a knight named Giovanni Gualberto, founder of the abbey of Vallombrosa. Thanks to him and his followers, the council of 1055 condemned "simony" and "concubinage" in the clergy, and in its name, in 1068, a monk who was a supporter of reform – called Fiery Pietro after this event – challenged the simoniac Bishop Pietro Mezzabarba to undergo ordeal by fire. The Bishop was forced to resign.

Behind the turbulent events of the eleventh century, in Florence no less than in Milan and other centres in the peninsula, men of the middle classes and of decidedly humble origins began to come to the fore, proudly taking part in the work of cleaning up the Church: laymen whom records of the time call, somewhat disdainfully, *patarini*. (The etymology of the word is uncertain, but it probably meant originally "rag and bone men" or "junk dealer"..) Not all of them came from such a modest background: reform was also supported by an aristocracy composed of people who worked with the Bishop, land owning knights and merchants.

The catalyst of these emerging classes was loyalty to the new Marchioness of Tuscany, Matilda of Canossa, who reigned for about forty years – from 1076 to 1115 – backing Pope Gregory VII's struggle against the Emperor Henry IV but also offering herself as mediator between them. Matilda's favour brought about the firm establishment of the city and its economy, and at the same time seemed to supply the basis of that which, viewed in a political perspective, was to be one of the "original characteristics" of Florentine history: loyalty to the papal cause and attention to the advantages it could bring.

By 1078 the population of the city had grown, and so had her military strength, but the people were aware that the clash between Pope and Emperor was going to bring hard times, and they therefore built a fourth circle of city walls; in other words they restored the perimeter of the third (that is, the Roman circle with the south-eastern addition) and joined to it, in order to protect the river port, the mighty castle of Altafronte on the Arno, in the area which today is occupied more or less by the Palazzo de' Giudici. On the opposite side of Florence, just outside the gate near the baptistery, stood

Matilda's residence: significantly adjacent to the city but outside its perimeter, as if to reassure its citizens that her authority would never weigh too heavily on it.

A city of warriors and merchants

Between the eleventh and twelfth centuries Florence was still a relatively modest centre compared with others in Tuscany. Although it was already clear that she was overtaking Arezzo, Volterra and other cities that were more illustrious in point of age, she was still decidedly inferior in point of population size, wealth and power to Lucca and Pisa, which also preceded her in acquiring free local government systems. Even nearby Pistoia and Prato still looked to the important centres of western Tuscany rather than to Florence; and the fact that the Via Francigena continued to bye-pass her was a disadvantage that had still not been overcome. The great Florentine buildings of the time – from the baptistery to the San Miniato monastery – with their strong, serene Romanesque lines and their characteristic combination of white and green marble, rendered homage to the aesthetics and technology of Pisa and Lucca.

Manufacture and commerce did not rise much above subsistence level; they did little more than satisfy the financial needs of the city, though there was a sign or two of coming opulence on the horizon, reflected in the beautiful religious buildings and perhaps supported by the aristocratic life of the families clustering round the House of Canossa and the Episcopal administration. Land was still the real backbone of Florentine wealth, in spite of the fact that the terrain was rough, hilly and here and there marshy and produced little in the way of cereal crops, though it did yield wine and olive oil (not highly esteemed for the table at that date).

Like the other cities of the Italian proto-Communal world, twelfth-century Florence set out to conquer the county, subdue the castles of the surrounding territories and gain ascendancy over the land-owning families and knights who dominated the territory from their strongholds. In the space of two years, between 1113 and 1115, the Cadolingi family, who controlled Valdarno to the west of Florence, petered out and the Countess Matilda died. Ten years after Matilda's death the Emperor Henry V also died, and there followed a long interregnum. Together these events facilitated Florentine opposition to the power of the feudal landowners who were among the supporters of the Emperor and of the Marquesses of Lorraine. They also made it comparatively easy for Florence to impose her will on smaller towns and cities.

It is symptomatic that in those decades one is much less conscious of the Florentine people than of their army. In 1125 the city expressed its unity for the first time in a firm collective action, the capture and destruction of Fiesole. Only the cathedral was spared, but the Bishop of Fiesole was forced to take up residence within the city boundaries of Florence. In the same way, as the castles were conquered and destroyed, the knightly families that owned them were obliged to become townspeople and live, for at least some months of the year, within what Dante called "the ancient circle".

Many ironical comments have been made on Dante's nostalgic memories of the Florence of that time, all sobriety and modesty. It is said that that sobriety was chiefly abject poverty, and that modesty first and foremost coarseness. Furthermore, it is asserted that the reactionary and factious Alighieri pretended to forget (and perhaps really was not entirely aware) that the Florence of that time "lived in peace" only up to a certain point. Towards the end of the twelfth century the city dominated the whole of the middle part of Valdarno, from Figline to Empoli, and had by now entered several times into direct conflict, or at least into some sort of close political relations, with the surrounding cities: Arezzo, Pistoia, Pisa and Siena. Among the powerful feudal lords who lived between the county of Florence and the counties of those other cities, only the Alberti to the north and west and the Guidi above all to the east could oppose her. But her ruling class contained families who came from the surrounding county and were proud of their warrior traditions; they had carried into the city streets the impregnable military buildings dedicated to their defence – the *case-torri* (house-towers, the towers that were dwellings as well as defence works) – and the custom of violence and feuding, that is, revenge.

By this time the Florentine county enjoyed peace and security, for the most part, because those who had once ruled it had not abandoned their possessions when they went to live in the city, but had seen that living together under the city's colours gave them a new collective strength.

This being so, trade was able to prosper: the easy river passage between Florence and Pisa – which between the towns of Fucecchio and San Miniato allowed a connection with the Via Francigena – was an excellent link with the outside world. A closely knit organisation of merchants, a "Guild", is on record as early as 1182. The budding Commune entrusted the maintenance of the beautiful great buildings such as the baptistery and the church of San Miniato, which were by now the very symbols of the city, to the merchants, although it did not allow them to take part in politics. Wide-ranging Florentine merchants bought cloth from Flanders and France, and precious dyes and alum from the Levant; they then had the cloth dyed in their workshops, so that they could re-export it at a heavily marked-up price. They combined commerce and manufacture with money-lending. This was risky, for they might at any time have been accused of usury by the Church, but it yielded a handsome and immediate profit. Trade, banking activities and the search for raw materials obliged the Florentines not only to travel continually but also to gather, assess and sort out information relating to the political and economic situation of various countries. In the twelfth century this was easy enough in ports, such as Pisa, Venice and Genoa; it was not usual, however, in inland cities, with the possible exception of Milan; so Florence was ahead of her time in enjoying this advantage.

But within the "ancient circle" the political climate was anything but peaceful. The institutions of the Commune were to take off not long after the deaths of Matilda and the Emperor Henry V, and hence to profit by the power vacuum they had left: the first verifiable piece of information about the existence of two consuls, however, goes back to 1138. Later the college of consuls increased to twelve; they took it in turns to rule, two at a time, and changed every two months, so that the whole year was covered. They were supported by a council of a hundred to a hundred and fifty *boni homines* (good men) and, four times a year, by a "parliament", an assembly of all the citizens of Florence. We do not know for certain what were the qualifications for taking part in the assembly, nor how it was conducted. Its function seems to have been to ratify the decisions made by the consuls and council; but what we know of the citizenry at that time, and of how any regime based on assemblies works, leads us to believe that it was the great families and their armed retainers who led the Commune.

The importation of stuffs and dyes, and the processing of textiles, admitted Florence to the trade circuits of Europe and the Mediterranean, but her trade nevertheless was dependent on access to ports, enabling her to receive raw materials and other goods and send out her finished products to foreign markets. As road transport was difficult, the Arno and therefore the port of Pisa were of the first importance to Florentines.

When, round about 1171, Pisa, in difficulty with Genoa and the Emperor, asked for help, Florence did not miss her opportunity: she did give military assistance – which cost her a long war against Lucca and Siena, who had allied themselves to the other side – but it was in exchange for substantial recompense in the shape of a share in the profits of the Pisan mint (and from that time the silver currency of Pisa became the Florentine currency too), the concession of favourable conditions for the transport of goods and of Florentine merchants on Pisan ships and for the payment of tolls in Pisan territory, and the availability of anchorage to Florentine merchandise in that prestigious port

The city's wealth increased in every direction; and so did the population, because the prospect of making money in the city attracted people from the rest of the county. They were not so much "fugitive servants", as has so often been said, as a robust class of property owners, people with solid assets, who, arriving in the city without, however, cutting themselves off from their roots, reinforced the domination of Florence over the surrounding country. It was guaranteed as much by the social participation of the *milites* turned city-dwellers as by their arms and castles. But the city was by now completely filled with stone, brick and wooden buildings.

The free spaces characteristic of urban centres in the late middle ages were used as orchards or even as small pastures, but by now they had disappeared under the welter of feverish building rendered necessary by circumstances. Newcomers settled along the roads which radiated from the gates towards the country, usually choosing to live where they could look out towards the places they came from. That was how the *borghi* (villages or suburbs) came into being, back to back with the "ancient circle", while a substantial residential nucleus grew up on the left bank of the Arno. Emporiums and workshops, but also the case-torri of notable families, had been built outside the walls, and it may be presumed that altogether the population was about 25,000. The threat of the Emperor Federico Barbarossa induced the Florentines to provide themselves hastily with new defences, for the most part wooden stockades, which enclosed the *borghi* too. The Emperor was determined to contain the independent cities and subdue if not crush them; moreover, there was tension between him and Florence's ally, Pisa, so her fears were not unfounded. The enormous task of bringing the *borghi* into the shelter of the city walls took from 1172 to 1175. They formed irregular triangles which had as a base the sides of the Roman perimeter walls. The new walls that included them maintained a shape that was very roughly quadrangular, but changed its orientation by about 45 degrees.

The city now had as its eastern limit the present-day Via de' Fossi (the course of the River Mugnone had recently been moved eastward) and the Trebbio gate was north of the present-day Piazza di San Lorenzo. There the walls curved towards the west, more or less to where the Arch of San Piero (all that is left of that part of the walls) now is. Turning south, they then reached the river again, after having encircled the entire area corresponding to the Roman amphitheatre, an area which previously lay outside the city limits. Later, in the early thirteenth century, three new bridges were built to connect the right bank of the Arno, where the city arose, with the left bank – that is, with the busy, turbulent, populous Oltrarno which from the

"Roman Gate" (as they then called what was later called Porta San Nicolò) extended as far as today's Porta Romana (known then as the "Porta di San Pietro in Gattolino") and Porta San Frediano. The road to Pisa started at that gate, running along beside the river. When the construction of the new defensive walls was complete, the area of the city, which in Roman times was 24 hectares, had risen to 75.

But with the enlargement and enrichment of the city came the loss of the peace, sobriety and modesty lamented by Dante. Things were not really as bad as he made out. The point is that the differentiation of the social and financial status of the citizens, the increased volume of trade and consequently the ever more quickly whirling circulation of wealth, the influx of aristocratic families and members of an upstanding middle class from the country had produced - with the growth of the city's dimensions - a considerable divarication and complication of social and political life. The appearance of consuls, from 1138, marks, among other things, the first definite proof that by then Florence had started on the road to city government. She was *de facto* independent, even if *de iure* subject to the sovereignty of the Roman-Germanic Empire, which had, however, since the death of Matilda, lacked the most important intermediate public institution, the marquisate of Tuscany. The consular type of government is always the product of a collective wish to rule on the part of a more or less extended group of aristocratic families who combine the practice of arms and the possession of land with a certain entrepreneurial bent for trade, which includes an ability to make use of connections with non-aristocratic entrepreneurs. The other side of the coin is the objective difficulty of collective government, and therefore a continual tension that bursts out from time to time in episodes of violence. Florence became a continual battlefield as a result of the use of arms, the existence in the city of belligerent buildings (the *case-torri*) inspired by the families' warlike past in the country, and the privilege of the right to carry on feuds, which set off a spiral of revenge until the entire ruling class was involved. What was at stake was power, and more immediately the mastery of one family by another. Family groups got together in actual "associations" (the statutes of some of them have survived) based on marriage, business dealings, friendship and neighbourhood. The neighbourhood concerned would be fortified by means of such connections between buildings as wooden galleries or passages which could be used or taken down at need.

The towers that crowned these fortifications could be as much as 130 "arms" (that is, 75 metres) in height. By the middle of the thirteenth century, Florence contained more than 150 of them. Little wonder that the family associations were called "tower societies". It is said that the impression Florence made then, with her centre surrounded by walls, must have been like the impression Manhattan makes today; but while that is true as far as the look of it is concerned, it must not be forgotten that that way of planning and building the city indicated above all that living there was like living in a fortress where the enemy was not outside by within.

Before long Florence's links with the rest of Italy and with the European and Mediterranean world ensured that the struggle between rival family groups became connected with wider reasons for conflict. The incursions of Federico Barbarossa and his allies into Italy in the third quarter of the century provoked various different reactions. The Florentine reaction, by and large (meaning that of the Florentine consular class), was to maintain a cautious line where Imperial policy was concerned, but in many episodes this caution turned into hostility. The Florentines had always shown unquestionable loyalty and formal respect towards the Holy Roman Empire, and would continue to do so until the end of the eighteenth century, but it was indeed a formal respect, a *fictio iuris* which, even though it had a high spiritual and cultural value and a deep juridical significance, meant little in the field of political decisions, which were determined rather by the complex network of alliances.

Moreover, since the direction of political decisions was determined by the group of family alliances that controlled the college of consuls, putting its members turn and turn about at the head of government, it was clear that the other groups, who felt excluded from it, aimed to get into it or to destroy its means of retaining power. Between 1177 and 1179 the precarious equilibrium of consular government was violently destroyed by a rebellion led by the powerful Uberti family, which from then on was accused of being seditious and enjoying the divisive support of the Empire, in the name of which it had rebelled.

In Florence, as elsewhere, the struggles between the Papacy and the Empire served as alibis to mask the internal struggles for power or to claim loftier and nobler motives for them. As time went on, however, these supposed motives acquired, in the partisan ardour of the conflict, a fascination and a fame destined to last and to have some effect on the practical plane.

The consular regime soon showed itself to be incapable of absorbing and containing these factious disturbances. Between 1193 and 1197 a new rebellion, provoked as before by the Uberti family, led, with the approval of the Emperor Henry VI, to its abolition. This time the Uberti had the support of many representatives of the merchant and craftsman classes, who had no reason to side with the consular establishment, having always been debarred by them from any form of participation in city government.

However, in practice the abolition of the consular system simply meant the substitution of one group of family alliances for another as rulers of the city; there was no real difference between the two, as to social composition, outlook or way of life. The consular system was re-established in 1197, once Henry VI was dead, but by then it was clear that the government of the city must be redefined on some new and different basis if it was to have greater stability.

Between 1197 and 1203 the Florentines embarked on an energetic series of actions aimed at consolidating the city's power over the county, especially in the south-west part of it, towards Valdelsa and the lower Valdarno; they were the key parts of the central Tuscan communication system, which included the Via Francigena and the River Arno. Meanwhile, consular government gave way to the system that depended on a *podestà*, the head of the Commune. The power which we would today call executive was in the hands of a single magistrate, who had, moreover, to be a foreigner because that seemed to offer a better chance of his being above factional rivalries. He had to be of the knightly class and to possess the qualities of a good leader in war. In his work as governor he was supported by a small council, which meant that the principle of the aristocratic college of consuls had been re-introduced into the new system. However, there was a second and larger council, whose members included the heads of the professional associations or guilds. (The Florentines called them *le Arti*.) From the fact that the *podestà* had to be a knight and possess both military ability and knowledge of the law (which could be acquired at the University of Bologna, attended by the sons of the great aristocratic families) it was clear that he had to belong to some noble house. The first *podestà* of Florence of whom we know anything was Gualfredotto da Milano, in 1207.

In the meantime something of the first importance happened: the social classes made up of shopkeepers and manufacturers, who in the traditions of the city were to become known as the (people), made their appearance on the scene. Ever since 1182 the merchants, excluded from sharing the consular power which was the monopoly of the aristocratic families, had founded a professional association on the model of the aristocratic groups. This was the origin of the body which was known as the *Arte di Calimala* (Guild of Calimala) because they had most of their shops in the "*calle maia*" (the widest street), which was based on the Roman cardo maximus. In the first twenty years of the thirteenth century other guilds had been formed: that of the bankers, the wool merchants, silk merchants (theirs went by the name of *Por Santa Maria* (St Mary's Gate), after the area in which most of the silk workers lived), and others too. All this conveys an impression of the vitality of the Florence of that time, and of the specialised sectors into which her economy was divided. That was a phase in which a sense of civic duty was splendidly fulfilled: the work to be done around San Miniato, the baptistery, the cathedral of Santa Reparata, the churches of San Pier Scheraggio and the Santi Apostoli were completed or at least substantially advanced. The decorative façades in bands of white marble from Lucca and green marble from Prato linked the aesthetic sense and taste of the Florentines with those of Pistoia and Prato and, through them, of Lucca and Pisa; but there is much in the detail and ornamentation of these churches to remind us that Florentine art bore, from the beginning, the imprint of the classical world, which was to continue and bear splendid fruit in future centuries. The mosaic facing of the baptistery interior, begun in 1228, sets a seal on the first of those great periods, so radiant with marvellous achievements, that made Florence into a city of art without parallel in the world.

But the entry of the "people" into the public and political life of the city, though not yet into participation in government, had done nothing to lessen the violence of the clashes between different factions of the dominant class. Usually, when something succeeded in briefly breaking the spiral of revenge which spread death and bitterness among the various family groups, there was a return to the old system of sealing new alliances with marriages, either to reinforce old bonds that had been broken or to create new ones. In 1216, during a wedding feast, a riot broke out between the members of two great families, the Buondelmonti and the Fifanti. To put an end to the incident, in which people had been hurt, the powerful Uberti offered to act as mediators. A Buondelmonti was to have married a daughter of the House of Amidei, allies of the family which he had injured in the course of the riot. Peace was made. However, his double-dealing or indecision led to more violence: after accepting the terms of reconciliation, he succumbed to flattery on the part of another great family, the Donati, and accepted their offer of one of their women as his wife, thereby setting off the inexorable sequence of revenge. The outraged Amidei, with their allies the Uberti and Lamberti, organised an ambush on the morning of Easter Day 1216, the very day on which the Buondelmonti-Donati marriage was to have taken place. Buondelmonti fell, arrayed like a sacrificial victim in his festive clothes and crown of flowers, at the foot of the ancient "statue of Mars", the pagan palladium of Florence, erected near the Ponte Vecchio. From then on, the old enmities were polarised and rationalised in two files: on one side the Uberti, the Lamberti and the Amidei, whose houses were all in the area in the centre of the city around the church of Santo Stefano in Ponte, between Ponte Vecchio and today's

Piazza Signoria, and on the other side the Buondelmonti, the Pazzi and the Donati, whose area lay between the present-day Via del Corso and Porta San Piero.

The warlike Ubertis raised this bipartite vendetta to a higher plane, linking it to the loftiest level of authority. Their loyalty to the Empire, which had shortly before returned to the House of Swabia, gave them the battle-cry *Weiblingen*! (from the name of one of the Swabia castles), and this led to their being called the "Ghibelline" party. Members of the opposing alliance were called the "Guelphs"; this was supposed to mean partisans of the House of Welf, that is to say the Duchy of Bavaria and later of Saxony, traditionally rivals of the House of Swabia. But at that time the House of Saxony, when Otto IV of Braunschweig died, had no hope of competing for the imperial crown. The term "Guelph", shorn of its original meaning, signified simply "anti-Ghibelline", and, as time went on and relations between the Pope and the Emperors of the House of Swabia got worse and worse, it came to mean "supporters of the pontiff".

For a long time the legend - dear to the *Risorgimento* and its romantic pseudo-history - continued that the Ghibelline party was composed of the nobles who were faithful to the Empire, reactionary and hostile to the liberty of the Commune, in the interests of a nostalgic plan to restore feudalism, while the Guelph faction were ranged - with the intelligent support of the Papal curia - on the side of all the good, honest and practical "bourgeois" entrepreneurs and manufacturers, who were tired of aristocratic privilege and feudal obstacles to the expansion of their activities. Unfortunately this legend persists in many school textbooks and works of popular history. Nothing could be further from the truth. Guelphs and Ghibellines originated as parties of the military nobility who derived the basis of their power, prestige and wealth from possession of *case-torri* in the city and land in the country, even if they did not disdain to take a hand in the trade and profits that could be extracted from them.

The "People", that is to say the manufacturers and entrepreneurs together, united in the Guilds, did not participate directly in the struggle between Guelphs and Ghibellines, although during the thirteenth century they were always deeply involved in it. They were quite distinct from the humbler classes of workers, who were employed in the various kinds of workshops. (These were the have-nots, whose wages barely reached subsistence level, a level often only attained with the help of almshouses and Church charities.) One reason for the involvement of the "People" in the struggles of their betters was the fact that their upper echelons were ambitious to achieve something like an aristocratic life style and allied themselves with families that were more distinguished in birth but short of goods and, above all, money. To be short of money was a serious disadvantage at a time when the circulation of money had become more and more rapid, the use of coin more and more necessary, and a share in the commercial and banking sectors more and more profitable. Together, these two groups formed a new class which united the pride, luxury and refinement of aristocratic customs with economic power derived from commercial and banking activities.

To this new class contemporary historical sources attribute names to which it is difficult to make precise and substantial outlines correspond, but which are, all the same, very expressive and eloquent: "the powerful," "the great people", "magnates". And terms like "greatness" and the verb grandeggiare (meaning both to tower or dominate and to put on airs) seem to have remained for a long time key words to describe not so much the elusive social and institutional substance of being "magnates" as the attitudes the magnates assumed, their way of behaving, of living, which was a mixture of warlike arrogance and chivalrous generosity, contempt for others and boasting, audacity and high-handedness.

But the Florentine dialect bears many signs of that tough period of life in the city, the era of the Commune, with its freedoms and its factions. Even today someone who does not have a clearly defined role in society, who does not have the energy to achieve a position and command respect, and who does not possess qualifications is said to have "*né arte né parte*" (to be good for nothing). Not being able to see yourself as part of some social or professional group, not having any party membership and therefor not having a direction to go in, an objective to aim for, is considered equal to having no part in the collective life of the city. Florentines have a name for the group and the faction within it: harking back to the terms which designated them in the past and have almost become archetypes in the collective memory, they call them *l'Arte* and *la Parte*.

The apogee

A complete "revolution of the road system" was brought about in the thirteenth century.

Thanks to the influence of its wide-ranging trades and to a series of firm military initiatives in the surrounding countryside, Florence, which had been cut off the Francigena, managed to reconnect to it through a land road system, thus forcing important trade to pass through its centre. By doing so, the town solidly and firmly conquered – thus replacing the power of the bishop – the surrounding countryside, subjecting it to the logic of its military needs and interests. At the same time it was however evident that the countryside was conquering the town, through a continuous flow of high quality immigration that conveyed inside the town individuals with capitals and initiative, who were ready to multiply their capitals by using their intelligence and daring.

Naturally enough, the increase and the greater articulation of economic activities attracted also growing throngs of underprivileged in search of work, drawn into town by the illusion of being able to rapidly and easily earn fortunes. A dream that would never come true in the vast majority of cases. Yet a great amount of cheap labour was exactly what florid factories and rich Florentine workshops needed. And on the other hand, feverish building activities, typical of a town in growth, were always desperately searching for labour at low cost.

This throng of underprivileged, which could be perhaps defined a sort of industrial working class, to use a strained interpretation, did not obviously find asylum in the centre dominated by aristocratic *case-torri* and embellished with large and beautiful buildings that already represented the true spirit of the town. Other miserable suburbs had already been built in unhealthy locations around the city walls in 1172-1175 (on the eastern and western banks of the river Arno, often on marshy and polluted lands).

These underprivileged classes were soon supported, aided and at the same time given a religious education by the mendicant orders, the new great reality of the 13th century that were specifically founded to meet the needs of the urban reality and "new poverty" originating from the commercial and entrepreneurial growth. Franciscans established themselves in the western area of the town, in the unhealthy area known as "Prato di Ognissanti", where a group of penitents – the "Humiliated" – started an activity linked with the production of wool, and in the eastern area where they founded the church of Santa Croce. The Dominicans established themselves close to the north-western section of the walls, in Santa Maria Novella. The Silvesters chose the northern side of the town, San Marco, which was later passed over to the Dominican order; the Serviti also established themselves in the north, in a suburban area surrounded by woods known as "Il Cafaggio", where they built the church of Santissima Annunziata. The Oltrarno, on the right bank of river Arno, was instead occupied by the Carmelites and the Augustians who respectively founded the churches of S. Maria del Carmine and Santo Spirito. In other words, the 13th century town was almost "encircled" by a circular chain of mendicant settlements, each characterised by a large church and by a wide square in front of it, which became necessary as a result of the increasing success of preachers and especially of Franciscan and Dominican friars.

Meanwhile the on-going strife between Guelphs and Ghibellines became more acute because of the participation of the noblemen of the country – mainly the families of the Guidi and the Alberti – and because of the wars against other Tuscan towns – mostly Siena and

Pisa – fighting for the hegemony of the region. The discontent for the corrupt behaviour of many clergymen created the ideal conditions for the flourishing of heretical propaganda. Apparently the 13th century Florence offered the Cathar sect the opportunity of propagandising a theological vision that strikingly contrasted Christian faith hidden behind a Christianity that was as pure and poor as in the origins, and appeared to be animated by the Neo-manichean principle of the struggle between the eternal principles of Good and Evil. Following the surge of controversies against the Papacy, the heresy apparently managed to gain the favour of some of the most important Ghibelline families and in particular of the Uberti. The Church responded to this attack with the mendicant Orders, which somehow joined charity and preaching, and with the Inquisition that was actually controlled by the very same orders (the Dominicans up to 1244 and later by the Franciscans of the Church of Santa Croce). The struggle between Frederick II and later between his son Manfred on the one side, and the Papacy on the other, radicalised the conflicts even within the boundaries of Florence. Here, as in many other towns, the opposition against heretics became more acute due to the strife against the Ghibellines and in some cases it actually became the same thing, also thanks to the Guelph propaganda. In 1244, the Dominican preacher Pietro da Verona galvanised a vast part of the population, who had adhered to the renewal stimulated by the mendicant orders and formed laic brotherhoods dedicated to devotion and repentance. The Ghibellines, who ruled the town at that time and included some members of the Cathar sect, responded by institutionalising the professional organisations and guilds that formed the People and by introducing two representatives to collaborate with the *podestà*.

Frederick II failed in his attempt to directly control the commune, even though his son Frederick of Antiochia, who became *podestà* in 1246, ruled the town with extremely harsh systems, managing to fight back a Guelph insurrection in 1246.

This was perhaps the first sign of the decline of the Ghibellines in town. Guelph exiles spread almost everywhere, together with a part of the wealth, but also with their prestige and friendships, and above all the Papacy. This facilitated the organisation of a counteroffensive. On September 21st 1250, in Figline, the Florentine army that had been patched together without too much conviction, was defeated in an ambush organised by the Guelphs. As the Guelph nobles in town had long since been exiled, guilds, that is the People, had to arm and upturn the tyranny. An unexpected insurrection in October 1255 marked the collapse of the Ghibelline regime and the permanent exile of the important families that had supported it.

It was the beginning of the most flourishing period in the history of Florence, which is also known with the name of the period of the *Vecchio Popolo* (Old People) or the *Primo Popolo* (First People). It is only an apparent ironical aspect of history that those who organised the insurrection against the Ghibellines ended choosing the same government institutions that the Ghibellines had created between 1244 and 1246. In reality nothing could have been more coherent. In both cases, entrepreneurs and Florentine merchants had reacted to decisions imposed from above and from foreigners, that is from the Papacy with the Inquisition first and from the Emperor through the Ghibellines later. While confirming their alliance with the Pope and keeping their distance from Manfred of Swabia (Frederick had died in 1250 and the throne had been vacant since 1254), the inhabitants of Florence were very careful not to call themselves Guelphs.

The institutional organisation of the government established after 1250 was characterised by two parallel bodies. The Commune on the one hand, ruled by the *podestà* and by two councils and the People on the other hand, directed by a Captain (who was also a foreigner and a knight like the *podestà*) assisted by other two councils. The former, formed by 12 members, was elected by the 20 military companies that represented the topographical areas where the citizens resided. The latter, formed by 24 members, was constituted by the consuls representing the Guilds. The captain and the "eldest" (that is the Council of the Twelve) represented the executive and legislative power, although the laws they issued had to be validated by the Councils of the *Podestà*. Although most of the Ghibelline aristocrats had been exiled from town, the Guelph ones – who had returned in 1250 – did not appear to be able to gain the favour of the people. It is true that they were used for several military and diplomatic actions and their prestigious relations with the Papacy, the feudal courts and most of the Italian signorias were often exploited. Yet, the Guilds were dominated by strong anti-aristocratic feelings; they could not forgive the "haughtiness" of the aristocrats and knew that they were dangerous because of their military strength. The "levelling" of the towers down to an height of 50 braccios, which was the equivalent of about twenty-five metres, was both a public order – because of the threaten of weapons that could be thrown down from them - and a moral and symbolic order.

The government of the "First People" was characterised by the extraordinary flourishing of the activities of the merchants and entrepreneurs of those Guilds that were later called the "Greater Guilds", which grouped importers of goods from foreign lands, bankers, wool manufacturers, silk manufacturers and fur and leather manufacturers. Their wealth influenced also the wealth of local merchants and craftsmen grouped in the so-called "middle" and "lesser" guilds. The newly established trades could rely on loans of large sums of money and contracts for the collection of Papal tithes. The necessity of maintaining the freedom of the countryside and of responding to the pressure of the neighbouring and nearly all Ghibelline towns – that hated Florence – led to the reorganisation of the military forces both on horse and on foot. These were divided into "sixths" or "wards" according to the new town districts. Even the town started to embellish itself. The *Palazzo del Popolo* (later renamed into *Palazzo del Podestà*, then *Bargello*) was built in 1255 in front of the Badia Fiorentina, followed by the bridge of Santa Trinità, five years later.

The necessary instrument to strengthen this economic growth would have been a prestigious currency. The Western world however did not mint coins, except for rather inferior silver ones, although the coins minted in Lucca, Pisa, Siena and Pavia were rather valued. Certainly not as much as the currency minted in Provins, which was used for trading purposes during the trade fairs of Champagne. As far as gold was concerned, gold coins were minted only in Byzantium and in some Muslim potentates. Emperor Frederick II had attempted to mint his own coin, the "Augustale", which did not however survive his death. In 1252, it was the turn of Genoa, who minted its "Genovino"; a few months later Florence triumphantly presented to the world its "Florin", a 23 carat gold coin weighing 3 grams and 55, which showed the image of John the Baptist on one face and the lily, the emblem of the town, on the other. It was the very same silver lily on a vermilion background represented on the ancient gonfalon with which the Ghibellines had fled and the People had decided to adopt, after "reversing" the colours into vermilion on a silver background, according to a typical heraldic opposition procedure. The "big Florin", or silver Florin, already existed. It was an important coin, whose value had been theoretically fixed at the time of Charlemagne as equivalent to 390 grams of fine silver. It was now decided that the gold Florin was to correspond to a value of 20 silver Florins, that is to a pound (or "lira"). As a matter of fact, the silver coin progressively and continuously lost value, while the value of the gold one remained unaltered for several years and actually acquired an enormous credit in the whole of Europe and in the Mediterranean area. The gap between the gold Florin and the silver lira had become so great, that towards the end of the 14th century a Florin amounted to 4 silver liras and to 7 silver liras at the end of the 15th century.

The Florin was obviously the currency used for important economic transactions; it was employed for the payment of large sums of money and for international loans. Entrepreneurs who traded using this beautiful and gold coin, usually paid their employees with inferior silver coins or in nature. By doing so they could make profit even on exchanges.

Nevertheless the situation of the government started to become critical when Manfred of Swabia – after eliminating his most prestigious Ghibelline enemy in Italy, Ezzelino da Romano, in 1259, deceased soon after because of the wounds suffered during the battle – thought it was time to conquer Tuscany and sent its officials to rule it. Florence could not obviously accept this hegemony and was consequently obliged to start a new war against Siena, whose ruling class formed by bankers was openly in contrast with the Florentine ones, Pisa and the exiled Ghibellines. The conflict broke out into a war that was settled for good with the battle of Montaperti, on September 4th 1960.

The Guelph army was exterminated, the "carroccio" – the symbol of the freedom of the Commune – was captured by the Siennese. The Ghibelline exiles returned to their town and fiercely put into practise their revenge, which consisted – as usual – in exiles, confiscation of property and destruction of houses rather than executions. However, when the Tuscan vicar of Manfred suggested, in 1264, to actually raze Florence, as Frederick I had suggested a century earlier, the acknowledged leader of the Ghibellines, Farinata degli Uberti, who was known to be a Cathar heretic, determinedly opposed the plan, "openly", as Dante quotes in his work.

The battle of Montaperti inaugurated a period of Ghibelline government, although it was difficult to set aside the Guilds, which had been cut out from the government of the town and from the exploitation of trades closely connected with the interests of Ghibellines. When Pope Urban IV excommunicated the Florentine and Siennese Ghibellines, in an attempt of reducing the power of Manfred and replacing him with Charles of Anjou, the brother of Luis IV, in Southern Italy, he authorised all good Christians not to pay the sums that had received as loans from the excommunicated. An order that was immediately obeyed. It was made clear that all merchants who declared themselves good Christians would have received a Papal document proving their faith, which would have allowed them to claim for their credits. Obviously enough, all or almost all the Ghibelline mercantile companies – even the Ghibelline ones – of Florence paid their homage to the Pope in the years between 1263 and 1264. This explains why the Florentine people found the courage to rebel against their domination and exile the Ghibellines after the defeat of Manfred in February 1266 in the battle of Benevento and the victory of Charles of Anjou.

Despite this political change, the government of the "First People" could never be restored. Although it soon became evident that the Florentine people were gradually acquiring specific Guelph characteristics, the Guelph movement and the people's movement were really never the same thing. Soon after the victory over Manfred, the Pope and Charles of Anjou, the new king of Sicily, clearly proved they had designs on this town of bankers, who had risked their capitals to allow the defeat of Manfred between 1263 and 1266. The "determined" representatives of the most important Guelph families, supported by two French knights of Charles, managed to impose their power and to appoint Charles as *podestà* of Florence for seven years from 1267.

The relation between Charles of Anjou and the Popes was always very troubled. The excessive power of the new king of Sicily in Italy and in the Mediterranean area was becoming rather worrisome. This explains why some Popes, like Nicholas III tried to limit it by supporting some of the fringes of the Ghibelline movement. Businessmen who still supported this view and had been exiled in Siena and Pisa obviously took advantage of this opportunity to restore their interests. As a consequence and as a result of a peace that was signed in January 1280 in Florence, thanks to the mediation of Cardinal Latino Malabranca, many Ghibellines were able to return to their homes.

It was only an artificial balance. The most important Ghibelline and Guelph families understood far too well that a conflict could not be avoided, since the stake was the rule over the town itself. The People, sticking close to the Guilds, were just waiting for the right moment to come and were determined not to be excluded as in 1260 and 1267.

Taking advantage of a new conflict that had broke out between the Guelphs and Ghibellines, the elders of the Guild of Calimala, the Bankers' Guild and the Wool Guild managed to have their representatives sit in the government of the Commune and gradually took over public functions through a council formed by six "priors of the Guilds", one for each district of the town. The change originated from the oath of loyalty made to the Tuscan communes by the new emperor Rudolf of Hapsburg, by the supremacy gained by the Ghibelline party in Romagna under the leadership of Guido da Montefeltro and by the "Sicilian Vespers" that had managed to shake the power of Charles of Anjou. At a later stage, the twelve "greater" and "middle" Guilds were authorised to elect a leader, arm troops and sit in the Council of the Podestà.

All these institutional changes took place in the two years from 1282 to 1284. Despite some turbulence yet without great upturns, the Guilds managed to impose a kind of government, which granted professional associations a greater power through the support of some of the most important Guelph families, the entrepreneurs and the bankers, assisted by local tradesmen and craftsmen.

This could not obviously meet the favour of the members of ancient noble families or of those were related or supported by these families, who shared their same political views and lifestyle. The strive between Guelphs and Ghibellines was gradually giving way to another kind of conflict between "magnates" and "lower classes", characterised by social rather than political issues. The Guelph magnate families, who were clearly aware of the fact that the core of their actual power and moral prestige lied in the use of arms, tried to solve the political disadvantage by again fomenting the strife against the Ghibellines, which had once more broke out in 1288.

The victory of Campaldino against the troops of Arezzo and the Ghibellines of Tuscany and Romagna, on June 11th 1289, gave the Guelph magnates the pretext to hope for a political rise. They asserted they had saved the town and imposed the entrance of St. Barnaba – on the same anniversary of the victory – in the Pantheon next to the ancient protectors of the town. The Guelph aristocracy was now the main enemy of the new movement that represented the middle classes, developed in the years from 1292 to 1295. Initially, its scope was to deprive the magnates of their authority, but it later focused on limiting their influence in the town life and on integrating their presence in a form of government controlled by the Guilds. The so-called "Ordinances of Justice" - a series of "extraordinary" ordinances issued in 1293 and emended into more moderate regulations in 1295 - established that the magnates could not be elected priors or become members of the Councils and provided for a series of very severe laws to protect the middle classes from their violence.

The "amendment" of '95 enabled some magnates to become members of the Guilds and actively participate in the government and in its organs. The new regime was somehow protected by a high magistrate of the Council of the Priors, called the Gonfalonier of Justice. Giano della Bella (a noble himself), who had been the leader of the middle classes since 1292, would have never accepted the presence of those magnates that the Ordinances had banned. For this reason, he was made to pay for his daring act and exiled. The truth is that Giano della Bella had clearly understood that the real danger for the People were the Guelph magnates. Yet, one should also remember that Florentine banks owed their wealth and prosperity to the alliance of the Guelphs with the Papacy, the king of France and the Anjou dynasty. In other words, the People had no other alternative and could not avoid making an agreement with the Guelphs to maintain their power and protect their prosperous trades.

After establishing that the magnates had to be deprived of all authority, it was a matter of deciding who the magnates were. These were not only represented by ancient noble families, who owned *case-torri* in town and other fortified possessions in the country. The term magnate identified anyone who could be suspected of threatening the power of the People in town because of his wealth, prestige and political actions. More than anything it was a matter of politics. The People decided which members of the several families were to be considered magnates and entered their names in special lists, from which they could also be cancelled. The first list of '93 identified 147 families, 73 of which lived in town and the remaining 74 in the country. At the later stage, the list of magnates would have included also members of the lower classes and of the People. The truth is that there was very little difference, in social and lifestyle terms, between the ancient noble families and less noble families that had become wealthy thanks to entrepreneurial and banking activities. The discrimination could only be political.

If we really want to understand the events that were taking place in Florence in this period, we necessarily have to look at other things besides constitutional changes. The events had led to the creation of a restricted class, constituted by ancient families and by the "new rich families" that actively contributed to growth of the economy of the town and aspired to an aristocratic lifestyle. Their scope was to gradually extend their hegemony over the government of the Guilds and to consolidate their trades by offering their support to the Papacy and to the French and Anjou dynasties, acting as bankers and tax contractors able to monopolise the whole European currency market.

The main instrument of this articulated mechanism was no longer the family group, but rather an organism that partially changed its form and spirit in time. This was represented by the banking and commercial company that was often named after the ruling family and that was generically referred to as the "company".

Each company was formed by a specific number of members (usually never more than twenty), who were often related to one another and who contributed with their shares to its capital stock. Companies obviously grouped both magnates and representatives of the lower classes. On the established expiry date, the company was cancelled and each member recovered part of the capital he has deposited, increased or decreased according to the profits or losses. Soon after a new company was established around the same ruling family with more or less the same members. At a first glance, companies appear to be very stable institutions without solution of continuity. The main "companies" in Florence, between the end of the 13th and the beginning of the 14th century, were those of the Mozzi, the Spini, the Scali and the Alberti, which were later joined also by the Bardi, the Acciaioli and many other families. The companies also managed currency deposits that were entrusted to them by small or medium speculators, who were not actually members of the companies themselves, and also by religious institutes (bishops, clergymen of the Florentine Chapter, who usually belonged to the most representative families in town and were therefore closely connected with this kind of business). International loans of very large sums were the most important and lucrative business of these companies that often carried out – through their foreign members and representatives – a very intense diplomatic activity. This is one of the "miracles" that helped Florence become what it is. This town where neighbours hated each other and where acute riots broke out for the sake of power or revenge, was able to inspire its citizens a great love.

The enemy Farinata degli Uberti had "openly" defended the town in front of this own party. Even the exiled families (like the Portinari, who had been exiled at the beginning of the 14th century) were considered very valuable economic, political and every-day allies for all those Florentines who happened to find themselves in the towns where they had been exiled, provided that they did not attempt to return into town by force. This explains why Florentines became – as was often said – the "fifth element" of the universe, from London to Paris, from Morea to Cairo, from Barcelona to Valencia, down to Byzantium and Cyprus.

This did not however attenuate the political conflicts. After the battle of Campaldino, the Guelph party had split into two different factions guided by the two families that fought for the government of the town, that is the Cerchi and the Donati. The former were the leaders of the so-called "white" Guelphs, the latter supported the "black" Guelphs. After a brief predominance of the white party – to which Dante Alighieri, Guido Cavalcanti and Dino Compagni also belonged – that was inclined to finding a peaceful agreement with the Ghibellines and resisting the hegemony of the Papacy (who was then represented by the strong and hierocratical Boniface VIII), the black faction overturned the situation with a bloody coup de man – with the support of Charles of Valois, the brother of the king of France, who had subtly offered his help as intermediary - exiling the representatives of the white Guelphs and confiscating their property. But harmony did not reign among the winners. The new threaten became the most prestigious and fascinating leader, Corso Donati who clearly had ambitions of extending his hegemony over the town. The black faction therefore attempted to sign a peace agreement with the white faction, until they both were defeated by the political and military power of the Tuscan Ghibellines who inflicted a very bad defeat to the Florentines first with the support of Emperor Henry VII and then of Ludovico VI and the prestigious leadership of Ugoccione della Faggiola and Castruccio Castracani.

Concerned for the evident political and military difficulties that could badly affect at any time their business, the exponents of the Florentine *Popolo grasso* (that is the most influent members of the families that controlled the Greater Guilds and the mercantile companies) asked for the help of Robert of Anjou, king of Naples, who was acknowledged as the international political guarantor. The king of Naples sent to Tuscany his son Charles, the Duke of Calabria, who was entrusted, in 1325 the signoria of the town for ten years. Unfortunately, the prince died soon after, in 1327, after partially relieving the military pressure from the town.

The half century that runs between the foundation of the "Commune of the Guilds" and ends with the signoria experiment of Charles of Calabria, coincided with one of the most splendid periods, from the architectural, artistic and cultural point of view. The town had enlarged and had now become one of the greatest and most populated towns in the West. At the end of the 13th century, its inhabitants were around 90,000 –100,000. New suburbs had been built outside the doors of the 1172-75 city walls. New city walls were built in 1282-84 on a project by Arnolfo di Cambio. Works were completed in 1333. The new city walls extended over a length of 8,500 metres, with 63 towers, enclosing an area of 630 hectares. It was only in the second half of the 19th century that the population reached and expanded beyond these city walls. The Florence of this period – of the *Dolcestilnovo*, of Dante Alighieri and of the final establishment of Italian as a language – was also the town in which Cimabue and his disciple Giotto renewed painting and Arnolfo di Cambio, a disciple of Nicola Pisano, gave new strength to architecture and sculpture; both solidly, distinctly and rigorously drawing their inspiration from ancient art. Some public buildings – both laic and religious – were built to add prestige to the town that was beginning to correct and rationalise its road layout, as you can see from the uniform and rectilinear line of Via Maggio and Via dei Serragli, on the south bank of river Arno.

The *Palazzo dei Priori* (Palace of the Priors) or *Palazzo del Popolo* (Palace of the People) was built in 1298 on the site that was originally occupied by the homes of the hated Uberti family, which had now been permanently banned. The palace, which faced a wide square, was later renamed into *Palazzo della Signoria* (Palazzo of the Signoria), although most Florentines simply called it *Palazzo Vecchio* (the Old Palace). With this configuration, dominated by the solid tower with a height of 95 metres, Arnolfo di Cambio clearly reinterpreted and summarised the past experiences of the *Palazzo del Podestà*. It was established that no other tower could have never been as high as the one of the palace, which symbolised the power and freedom of the Commune. Over the same years, Arnolfo di Cambio also completed the marble decoration of the baptistery and conceived a modular ratio that could balance this building and the new cathedral, which was built over the remains of the ancient and small church of Santa Reparata. The new religious building clearly drew inspiration from the Cistercian gothic though its verticalness was corrected in order to adapt it to the breezier Florentine taste.

The project of Arnolfo was completed in 1296 and followed by the building of the new cathedral, which was dedicated, as all the large cathedrals in Europe, to the Virgin Mary, Santa Maria del Fiore. Arnolfo, who also drew the projects for the churches of Santa Croce and of the *Loggia del Grano* (best known as *Orsanmichele*) is the genial artist, who managed to reconcile the Romanesque inheritance – think of the church of San Miniato – with the new Gothic taste, tending towards a classic renewal that would have later been fully interpreted by Brunelleschi and Alberti. This was also the time in which new religious complexes were built, like the church of Santa Maria degli

Angeli close to Santissima Annunziata, together with the beautiful palaces of the ruling class, like those of the Frescobaldi, the Spini, the Gianfigliazzi - close to the bridge of Santa Trinita - and the palace of the Peruzzi, characterised by a curved facade that reminds us of the ancient layout of the Roman amphitheatre once located in Santa Croce. The ruling class commissioned the erection of grandiose chapels with pompous frescoes in churches like Santa Croce, Santa Trinita, Santa Maria Novella and Santo Spirito to symbolise, in each quarter, their power outside the walls of churches and of their palaces.

This was the Florence that Dante condemned, with its "newly arrived families", its "ready-at-hand profits", governed by anger, envy and avarice. A Florence dominated by unrestrained luxury and by shameless women wearing make-up and very low necklines. It was the town that had discovered the power of money and the heroic, and sometimes dangerous, initiative of avid, intelligent and even cruel men, who stuck close their families, their factions, to the water of the river Arno and to the stones of a city that was becoming larger every day. Of men who dreamt of conquering the whole world.

Crisis and redefinition of a "bourgeois" city

Angelo di Bondone, known as Giotto, had already started building his famous bell tower before his death in 1337. Almost in the same years, Andrea Orcagna was building the airy loggia next to the *Palazzo dei Priori* and Francesco Talenti was starting the construction of the new *Orsanmichele* with his loggia characterised by ogival arches and columns.

These three building are almost a symbol of perfection, aligned along the line of Via Calzaioli, and the celebration of a "bourgeois" class that appeared to be making its way in town.

This is the town of the joyful group of storytellers featured in the *Decamerone*. The young and joyful group of people portrayed in the frescoes in the cemetery of Pisa, who are playing around in a beautiful garden unaware that death is ready to step in. The truth is that the ruling class substantially failed to fulfil its scope.

Between the thirties and forties of the 14th century, the Mozzi, the Frescobaldi, the Spini, the Bardi, the Peruzzi, the Acciaioli and the Bonaccorsi were busy lending money – at high rates and with very high risks – to the Popes of Avignon, the kings of France and England and to almost all the most important princes in Italy and Europe. Florentines refined and practically manufactured directly almost 7-10% of all the wool cloths manufactured in the West, importing and consuming incredible amounts of allumen and precious dying substances. Florentines gave work (although very badly paid) to the vast majority of the underprivileged classes of the town and of the country, since the processes that transformed wool into precious and soft cloths required almost thirty different stages. Bankers, traders and manufacturers supported each other. The Guild of Calimala and the Wool Guild were, together with the Bankers' Guild, the Guilds that dominated the town.

And yet this castle of skill and wealth had very weak foundations. In the 14th century the military defence Florence could oppose was very weak and easily defetable. In the first quarter of the century it had badly been defeated by the Ghibellines, as for instance during the battle of Montecatini that had compromised its prestige. A strong army was exactly what it needed, especially at a time when Florence was no longer the centre of principality-town, but was becoming the centre of a regional state. Florence dominated in fact several minor centres and even other towns, like Prato, Pistoia and later also Arezzo. Its territory stretched south towards Valdarno, Pisa, the Chianti valley, Valdelsa and Siena and north towards Valdarno and the Apennines. "New lands" and new centres were being established especially in Valdarno and in the mountain area. Although Pisa and Siena had surrendered and abandoned their Ghibelline faith, thus adapting their governments to the wishes of their rival, Florence never managed to lay its hand on Lucca, even though the latter was experiencing a critical situation and often entrusted his freedom to casual and unreliable patrons. The Hundred Years War that broke out in France and the news of the insolvency of the English king Edward III, to whom the companies had lent large sums of money, initiated a sequence of chain bankruptcies that impoverished the town. In 1311 the Mozzi were ruined, followed soon after by the Scali in 1326. In 1333, a frightful flood – that also carried away the statue of Mars on one of the sides of the Old Bridge, a most unlucky omen – seemed to anticipate the disaster that was about to hit Florence. The families of the Bardi, Peruzzi, Acciaioli and the Bonaccorsi were practically ruined in the years between 1342 and 1346. The families managed somehow to save part of their wealth or to reconvert it into land and castles, transforming themselves from merchants into noblemen living in the country in a kind of feudal environment. Middle and small savers, who had entrusted their modest capitals to these families to profit from their investments, were however totally ruined. And it was to these men that Florence owed its prosperity.

To solve this emergency situation, which had also created a certain degree of political instability, the ruling class decided to entrust the signoria of the town to a French nobleman, who had carried out successful campaigns in the East and knew Florence, having visited it in 1325-27 as a follower of Charles of Calabria. This man was Gualtieri of Brienne, (supposed) Duke of Athens. The ruling class that had appointed him soon became suspicious of this attitude, as the duke's policy appeared to be a mixture of arrogance, personal and disputable decisions and superb knightly attitudes. Well realising that he was in the hands of those who had given him the power, Gualtieri tried to gain an independent group of supporters by showing his favour to the working class and especially to the workers of the Guild of the Wool (the so-called "wool-combers"). In other words, he attempted to gain the favour of the "Lesser People" who were not part of the Guilds and were obliged to live on the low salaries paid by the merchants and owners of the enterprises. The salaries were so low that they often hardly managed to survive and often had to rely on the food and clothing distributed by the many hospices in town to live.

Due to his open sympathy for the working class, and not so much because of his tyrannical and capricious attitude, the Duke of Athens ended in loosing his power. The noble families and the wealthy merchants who had called him organised a complex and competitive system of plots aimed at eliminating him. The day on which the Duke was overturned – July 26th 1343 – became the Day of St. Anne, one of the main festivities of the political and religious calendar of Florence. This festivity was celebrated in the church of Orsanmichele, the Pantheon of the Florentine Guilds.

The festival of St. Anne did not so much celebrate the recovery of freedom, but marked the return of the power in the hands of the *Popolo Grasso*, made possible also thanks to the support of some magnate families, who were highly regarded because of their services and were allowed to sit in the councils of the town. It was obvious by now that the town was ruled by a signoria and that the main organs were the Gonfalonier, the Eight Priors, the Council of the Good Men and the Council of the Sixteen Gonfaloniers of the Guilds. The priors were eight and the guild gonfaloniers were sixteen. They both represented the whole town that had been divided into new quarters. By now, the division according to trades had been finally abandoned and the town had been split into four quarters named after the main churches (Santa Maria Novella, San Giovanni, Santa Croce and Santo Spirito).

Quarters had their own gonfalon. Gonfalons were important units for fiscal and military purposes, although the town usually employed mercenary armies for its defence.

The difficult political and financial conditions, including the defeat of Montecatini and the exile of the Duke of Athens – that correspond to stagnant situation characterised by a very low demographic and economic growth in the whole of Europe and in the Mediterranean area – interrupted the development or at least reduced the growth of all the activities of the town. Between the end of the winter and the spring of 1348, Florence was hit by the plague that had broke out a year earlier in the regions of the Black Sea spreading over the whole continent. It is difficult to give figures on the Plague. Apparently it reduced the population of Florence by 40-60%, as in most European towns. More pessimistic estimates calculate that the population of about 120,000 people at the beginning of the 14th century was reduced – after the Plague – down to 25,000 – 30,000 inhabitants. According to other calculations, which are rather approximate due to lack of reliable sources, the population was reduced by a number ranging from 90,000 – 100,000 to 50,000 people.

The number of inhabitants raised to 70,000 people in the last twenty years of the century and decreased down to 40,000 people around 1427, when cadastral sources offer us more reliable data. In the years that followed, the population of Florence reached about 80,000 inhabitants and started to slowly and continuously grow after the end of the recurrent plagues, that is between 1348 and 1630. The inhabitants raised to above 100,000 units only after Italy was reunited. In examining the frightful figures of the plague, we have take into account that not everyone died because of the plague. Many had preferred to flee to the country, believing that they would have been less exposed to the plague, and ended preferring the country to the town. The plague had in fact improved the wealth of the country areas and somehow opened the way to land speculation. The reduction of labour, both in town and in the country, obviously affected the social, economic and political life of the Florentines. It should in fact be remembered that plagues were often followed by famines, according to a well-known chain sequence. The situation was then worsened by the on-going wars and by the continuous and damaging invasions of mercenary armies, which were employed by almost all the Italian towns at very high wages to fight endemic and rather useless battles. In other cases, towns actually paid the mercenaries to keep them out of their territory. Compared to the lively 13th century, the 14th appears to be poorer and more neurotic.

As a result of these events, Florence, like many other towns in the northern and central Italy, experienced a series of riots organised by the underprivileged classes, who really lived in very miserable conditions. Their scope was not a social revolution. Their only aim was to be included in the recognised professional associations and acquire the right to be recognised as body (we must remember that they could not even join religious brotherhoods). They did not want to overturn the order imposed by Guilds, but rather be admitted to the guilds and participate in them. On the other hand, the noble families of Florence carefully watched the situation, ready to strike back at any attempt that would have deprived them of their authority. For this purpose, the new election system inaugurated in 1343 was controlled by a complex series of *imborsazioni*, which consisted in a random selection of the names of the citizens who were assigned public offices. The names were inserted in special bags (from the Italian word *borsa*) and then extracted. Sometimes the elected citizen did not meet the favour of the ruling class. In this case, his name was cancelled from the lists of the citizens who had a right to be elected, with a typical system called *ammonizione* (admonition), following the decision of a special council, the so-called *Parte Guelfa* (Guelph party).

The *Parte Guelfa* was the stronghold of the important families who most resolutely opposed changes. It had the power of proclaiming "Ghibellines" and therefore of "admonishing" those whose political prestige appeared to grow excessively and all those who did not belong to the trustworthy group of oligarchs. Naturally enough, influent citizens who felt cut out from the group or kept at too much of a distance – like the Duke of Athens for example – often attempted to find a core of supporters within the underprivileged or more miserable classes. The quarter of the century from 1350 to 1375 was characterised by the struggle between the "Middle Classes" who held the power and a large and composite group that included some noble families, several members of the new stock that had recently arrived in town to replace the space left vacant by the plague, down to the "populace". In 1375, as a consequence of a food-rationing crisis, a *signoria* principally ruled by the "Middle Guilds" and supported by a certain extent by "populace", perhaps because of the common goals, started a war against the Apostolic Legates, who were preparing the return of the Pope from Avignon both in northern and central Italy. The conflict obviously draw on Florence an interdict. The inhabitants of Florence replied obliging their clergy to continue celebrating their masses and proudly claimed their religiousness in an almost choral and indignant reaction against the clergy who used religion as a political instrument.

The eight magistrates "responsible" for organising the war were named "The Eight Saints". Thus, Florence responded in its own way to the interdict of the Pope. The conflict that lasted until 1378 was referred to as "The War of the Eight Saints". Apparently during the conflict and in the years the preceded and followed it, some partially heretical groups, like the so-called "small friars", who preached a poor church and a return to the Christianity of the origins, incited the Florentines to rebel against the Papacy and the corrupt clergy, obtaining a large consensus especially from the underprivileged and poor classes.

On the other side, even the oligarchy that supported the Guelph Party and the Greater Guilds had its own form of spirituality. The most important personality in this sense was the inspired Caterina Benincasa, who never ceased to invite her Florentine disciples to work towards a peace between Florence and the Papacy.

The conclusion of the "War of the Eight Saints" threw into bold relief the role of the "populace". In July 1378, the "Ciompi", that is the wool-combers raised in a "tumult" with the aim of raising their salaries and obtaining better life conditions, but also of achieving a judicial and institutional recognition of their status. The tumult led to the creation of three new Guilds, called "Guilds of the People of God", to represent the tailors, dyers and wool-workers. Between 1379 and 1382, however, the "Middle Classes" managed to maintain their unity and oppose the new Guilds (this was easily done due to the opposed interests the new guilds). Later, they had to recourse to force to overcome the new political situation and remove from power a four-year government that appeared to be sensitive to the more modest classes. A new oligarchic regime was again established. The struggle for power set aside social issues to become once again a strife between the great noble families. The new protagonists were the Albizzi. By alternating violence to a control over the electoral lists and leading a vast group of families directly connected or devote to them, the Albizzi managed to defeat each time the opposed family groups (who unlike this family did not base their consensus on a dominant oligarchy, but on underprivileged classes). They therefore defeated the Ricci and the Alberti, until the struggle radicalised and affected more directly the circle of the Albizzi. The conflict saw the opposition of the Albizzi, representing the old oligarchy, and the Medici, who were widely supported by the newly arrived citizens and by the representatives of the "middle" and "lesser" guilds.

Meanwhile, the sphere of influence of the republic was extending over the rest of the region. Between the end of the 14th century and the beginning of the 15th, Florence was forced to sustain a very hard war against the Duke of Milan, Giangaleazzo Visconti, who wanted to extend his dominion in central Italy through the co-operation of his many supporters. Romantic historiography, enchanted by the high eloquence of the chancellor of the signoria, Coluccio Salutati, who celebrated with Ciceronian Latin and Roman dignity the liberty of Florence, really believed that the conflict between the town of the lily and the "Count of Virtue" was a strife between freedom and tyranny. In reality we have already seen that Florentine freedom was intended mainly as independence from higher institutional bodies (like the Emperor), but never really pursued the ideals of freedom or equality on behalf of its citizens. It represented above all the freedom or rather the power of the oligarchs of the town. As far as the other towns in Tuscany and the smaller communities were concerned, chancellor Salutati preached a freedom that did not exist. The tyranny of the Visconti in the Po valley was generally less harsh, fiscal and rapacious and more respective of local autonomy and traditions than the so-called Florentine "freedom". These considerations must naturally take into account that the "regional state" of the 14-15th century was notn centred and levelled from an absolutist standpoint, since it was more of a constellation of specific situations, a set of bilateral agreements between the dominant town and each of the centres and ruling bodies, with a wide variety of specific cases.

Yet the appeal of Salutati to the republican freedom of ancient Rome was a synthesis of the political course developed by Florentines and the sense of the new times to come.

Dante informs us that even in the virtuous age when Florence was still encircled by the "ancient walls", mothers used to tell their sons stories about the "Trojans, of Fiesole and ancient Rome", that is of the ancient origins of the town, which, according to the legend, were also celebrated in the 14th century both by historians (Villani and Malispini) and poets (in the Ninfale by Giovanni Boccaccio). It was generally acknowledged that Florence was the first daughter of Rome and that the blood of the

Florentines was either the one inherited by the generous Julius Caesar or – as in the case of the Uberti – of the seditious Catiline. Old and rather provincial legends, originating from an attempt of vulgarising history, reduced the stories of Livius and Tacitus freeing them from their Latin solemnity and freely transcribed into a more vulgar language that could be understood by merchants and craftsmen. In this town of merchants, the subjects studied were mainly the abacus, mathematics and accounting. There were also "reading schools" where pupils learnt "grammar" and therefore also Latin. As many towns populated by businessmen and characterised by on-going strives and conflicts, Florence was crowded with "judges" (lawyers) and notaries, who formed all together one of the Greater Guilds. It is worth noticing that the University of Florence was late in developing; practically it did not develop before the 15th century.

The young students of Florence seeking a degree in law o medicine had to go to Pisa, Siena, Bologna and in some cases as far as Padova. This fact however helped to preserve Florence from the boring and often sterile disputes of the dying scholastic philosophy and open it to a new culture that developed free from all prejudices. Judges and notaries could read Latin and expressed themselves with sobriety and elegance in this language in the councils and chancellor's offices of the signoria and every time it was necessary (as in the case of official documents), drawing inspiration directly from ancient models. At the beginning of the 15th century, a group of scholars closely linked to some of the fringes of the ruling group of the time – the Albizzi – decided to organise a sort of study centre that rivalled the official one, centred on scholastic philosophy. They chose, for this purpose, the convent of Camaldoli of Santa Maria degli Angioli and started promoting from this centre a new teaching and learning system, based on the free discussion of texts like the Ciropedia of Xenofon. In this centre, classic works were read and discussed without too many mediations (and "commentaries"; "glosses" represented the most important instrument of scholastic education). Particularly important were the subjects being discussed. Xenofon, as large part of the works of Cicero, were not about theology or philosophy. They were about politics, the art of governing and described the techniques to educate the youths who would have later taken up public offices.

This focus on a more practical and political knowledge also expressed the need of discovering the world. Many have often wondered why this rational and positive town of bankers and merchants attributed so much importance to astrology. A question of this kind obviously means making a big mistake and interpreting facts from a modern point of view. The favourite astrology of Florentines, who – like most other peoples – never chose a commander or erected a building without scrutinising the position of the stars, was not a cold and arid science that subdued man and his capacities to the impersonal power of stars. On the contrary, it was used to find the most propitious time to inaugurate a palace or sign an agreement, start a journey or a job. The subtle and complex relations between the stars and the earth and the knowledge of the laws that govern them were continuously exploited from a practical point of view in order to increase wealth, improve health and grant success.

The true and great universality of Florentines did not lie in the University, the jewel of the archbishop Antonino (Florence had become in the 15th century an archdiocese), but in the world. The manuals specifically written for merchants – like the *Practise of Trading* by Francesco di Balduccio Pegolotti – focus on worldly issues and describe in detail ports, roads, caravan routes, goods, prices and currency exchange. But also the journals written by missionaries like Ricoldo da Montecroce and Giovanni de' Marignolli or by pilgrims like Lionardo Frescobaldi and Alessandro Rinuccini, are full of information on Egyptian and Syrian markets and traditions. Even chivalry novels, which were to some extent a very popular genre – it is sufficient to think of Guerrin Meschino by Andrea da Barberino – speak about journeys showing a mixture of imagination and a true and genuine curiosity for distant worlds.

Chivalry adventures were popular in this world of businessmen and tradesmen. Naturally enough, at the end of the 13th century, the ruling class began showing a great of attention to war decorations and attributed a great importance to the sumptuous ceremonies for the clothing of knights, heraldic signs, tournaments and jousts. Story tellers and moralist always found the right opportunity to make fun of these people, who loved weapons and parades, despite their little courage and scarce military ability. It is evident that their love for these topics externally and symbolically represented a process that has been termed refedaulisation, using perhaps a far too schematic expression. The merchants and bankers, who had already experienced the economic and financial crisis of the forties in the 15th century, had hastily invested their capitals in estate (good land never lets you down), thus partially transforming themselves into *rentiers* and acquiring also their characteristic behaviour and "lifestyle", that is feudal and signoria-like attitudes. It is useful to remember that between the 13th and 14th centuries, Florence was closely linked to the cultures of the Po valley, France and Burgundy, which inspired the "Gothic-Flemish" style – from the late paintings of Giotto, Masolino da Panicale down to Beato Angelico himself – that so much appreciated by the ruling class. It is also worth remembering that the gilded silver spurs and the ermine mantels that distinguished knights were the credentials needed to prove one's power in foreign towns and rule in the position of *podestà*. But there was more to come.

Adventure tempted Florentines. Let's leave aside Pazzino dei Pazzi, who was said to have participated in the first crusade and brought back to Florence some of the stones of the Holy Sepulchre.

This is a legend. A true event - although it seems a kind of legend - was the story of the Acciaioli and Buondelmonti in the East, who took over a large part of Greece and lived like feudal lords in their new territories.

Even the story of Filippo degli Scolari ("Pippo Spano") is a true story. At the beginning of the 15th century he became one of the most powerful lords of Hungary. Niccolò Acciaioli and Pippo Spano, the protagonists of this new Florentine '*Drang nach Osten*' (call to the West) would have had the honour of being portrayed by Andrea del Castagno in the gallery of the most important historic personalities, which the Pandolfini had commissioned for the villa of Legnaia (these frescoes are today preserved in Florence in the Cenacle of Santa Apollonia). This gallery features figures taken from sacred history (Esther), Roman history and myths (the Cumean Sybille, Queen Tomiri), but also Farinata degli Uberti, Dante and Boccaccio. Florence responded to the Gothic tradition of the '*cycle of preux*' based on Biblical subjects and on knights of the Charlemagne and Breton cycles, with the practical biography of heroes, who followed the models offered by Plutarch. It was not a sheer chance if Filippo Villani, the descendant of a lineage of story-tellers who wrote in vulgar, soon started his *De viris illustribus urbis Florentiae*, in which his admiration for the gestures and works of ancient Romans was integrated with the desire of exalting his own town and establishing a canon of Florentine civic virtue.

In passing from the "free" commune of Dante, characterised by political and social conflicts, to the oligarchic republic that gives birth to Renaissance, artistic and cultural issues suffer a kind of reduction, which originates from the loss of freedom and the concentration of wealth and power – originally distributed among a vast ruling class – in the hands of few families. A judgement of this kind would appear to be influenced by an ideological prejudice. In reality in fact, the Florentine oligarchy definitely adopted a discretionary and selective attitude even towards the artistic and cultural works it promoted and commissioned after overcoming the crisis of the forties.

There is no doubt, for example, that after the period of consuls and *case-torri*, where the interests of the guilds appeared to prevail over the public ones, the flourishing of Florence in the 13th and 14th centuries was significantly influenced by a political and public element that affected all the masterpieces of the period, from the *Divina Commedia*, the *Palazzo dei Priori* down to the new cathedral. Likewise, the 15th century Renaissance privileged a literature and an art that – after the season of Salutati, Bruni, Bracciolini and of a politically committed "civil Renaissance" – objectively served the will and whims of the important families, preferring mythological subjects to political issues, idyllic topics to civic subjects, the mystic or commemorative works destined to adorn churches and private altars of individual families to the practical religiousness of the Guilds and of local brotherhoods. This is only apparently true. In reality the rhetoric and commemorative function of this literature and art is deeply connected to a process – that is far from evasive, yet rather practical and political – that privatised the state. The result of this process will be the signoria and later the principality of the Medici. It is impossible not to understand the deep political traits of works like *The Cavalcade of the Magi* by Benozzo Gozzoli in the Medici palace of Via Larga or The *Old Sacristy* of San Lorenzo.

On the contrary, it is true that without the crisis of the middle 14th century and the oligarchic reaction to the tumult of the "Ciompi", the new aesthetics, largely inspired to the wide-ranging and relaxed rhythms of Roman art, would have not been able to develop due to the lack of urban spaces and of customers constituted by the large families.

The journeys of Brunelleschi and Donatello to Rome, from 1402 onwards, reflect a new way of conceiving the town, the palaces of the noblemen and space. Without the plagues that had reduced the walls of the 13th-14th century town to an excessively large clothing for a town that had lost most of its inhabitants – who had abandoned buildings now ready to be purchased and demolished and replaced by noble palaces, in addition to non cultivated lands that could be used as gardens – the Renaissance architecture would have not developed so easily.

Meanwhile the Florentines had conquered Pisa in 1406 and the port of Livorno in 1421. At this point they were able to put into practise an old dream and start an independent maritime activity. In almost the same years, the *Cosmography* of Tolomeo had reached the town and was being translated. It was a new call to gain possession of the world. Trading needs, love for trading, but also an artistic respect for geography and mathematics were now starting to mingle with the dream of adventures. The road was opened to Paolo Toscanelli and Amerigo Vespucci.

A town for the prince

The wealthiest family of Florence in the early 15th century was undoubtedly the Strozzi family. Yet the most powerful family, opposed by the Medici bankers, were the Albizzi who were at the head of the strong Guild of Calimala that had branches almost everywhere in Europe and in the Mediterranean and could rely on the most prestigious and efficient political and diplomatic network of friendships in town, as it financed popes and kings. The struggle for power was often very fierce, although it involved in the first place the constitutional play of "imborsazioni" and "admonitions", through which contenders disputed the supremacy of government bodies, in addition to the usual endemic spiral of violence and revenges.

The struggle for power between the Albizzi and the Medici is somehow connected to the institution of the land register, that is to an organic taxation system based on capitals and incomes on both estates and assets. Before then, the revenue of the Commune was based mainly on a confused system of indirect taxes and on some "assessments" or rather taxes on property. Practically, public finance relied prevalently on duties and "tolls" applied on the goods in transit and on the commune's assets.

When particularly high sums were needed, the State appealed to the so-called "prestanze" or rather loans that could be compulsory or voluntary. The return mechanisms connected with the loans became in time so burdensome that it was necessary to establish a "pawn agency" in 1343, that is a form of consolidation of the public debt that allowed big speculators to rely make a big profit from "state bonds" at an increasingly higher interest. In 1358 public debt bonds were offered at three hundred florins in return of one hundred florins in cash.

Everyone in Florence practically paid the same share of taxes – both the rich and the poor – on consumables, while the public debt system simply drained money to the advantage of the wealthiest. In 1427, the expenses originating from the long-lasting wars against the Visconti – the stake was, once again, the conquest of Lucca – had become so exorbitant that it was necessary to appeal to a taxation system that finally drew money from where it was available. In other words, from the treasuries of the wealthy families. The supporter of the new land register was the head of one of the fighting factions, Giovanni de' Medici, who by doing so undoubtedly exposed himself – together with many friends and allies – to high duties. It is to no use objecting that this action negatively affected also his enemies, leaded by the strong Rinaldo degli Albizzi. But Giovanni, whose family had been following for over 50 years a policy aimed at gaining the favour of the lower classes of the town. The fact was that humbler people and middle-class entrepreneurs were tired of the on-going dispute with Milan, of the high expenses of the war and of the fact that the "burden" prevalently affected the humbler classes, leaving the wealthy families to speculate on the public debt. His action was political and perhaps even demagogical, not certainly financial.

After the death of Giovanni in 1429, the leadership of the family, of the company and of the Medici faction passed on to his son Cosimo. In 1433, Rinaldo degli Albizzi managed to accuse him of the failure of the campaign against Lucca, declare him magnate and exile him in Padova. Cosimo had however powerful friends and good reserves of capital both in this town and in Venice. During this period he managed to change the exile in an opportunity for carrying out his political and diplomatic plan. About a year later, in 1434, he was called back to Florence by a *signoria* favourable to him. It was the turn of the Albizzi and of some of their allies to be declared magnates and be exiled.

It was the beginning of the fortune of the Medici family, which was destined to rule Florence for over three centuries, although in different positions and with alternate episodes. Cosimo was said to dislike behaving like a prince and always governed the town and the state as a private citizen. He seldom participated in the government organs (that were called at the time *signori e collegi*) and was satisfied to manage the electoral lists and place his friends and clients, generally mediocre characters, in key positions. It is evident that the signoria of Cosimo – the last to be established, at a time in which most of the Italian signorias had already been transformed into principalities – bears no trace of the war-like and feudal characteristics of the signorias established in the Po valley, in Romagna and Marche.

Cosimo continued to faithfully believe in the ancient Roman model of the good citizen who may occasionally access the *cursus honorum*, yet prefers to follow the *negotia* of his home and of his business and take advantage of the otia offered by the villas and studies, in which he does not excel yet he greatly estimates and generously promotes. He is well aware that patronage is a good political investment; it places in the foreground the patron and his family; it obliges others to talk with admiration about the patron; it mobilises intellectual and economic forces; it creates moral debts and gratitude that are just as useful as economic debts in politics.

He was been termed by many as "cryptolord" and was known to rule his state from "the back rooms of his house in Via Larga". This is true, but it is also true that his house in Via Larga was in reality a large palace with a view over the beautiful San Giovanni and the parish church of the Medici family, San Lorenzo, the venerable sacred basilica that preserved the vestiges of St. Ambrogio, symbolised the establishment of the Christian identity of Florence and was later destined to become the church representing the glories of the Medici family. It is also true that the ambassadors of the Pope, of the emperor, of the most important kings of Europe and of the Italian states usually visited the home of Cosimo in Via Larga and talked about the most important matters, after a more or less hasty homage visit to the Palace of the Priori (or some cases before the visit itself).

The core of the strength of the Medici family lied in the greatness of the Guild of Calimala, which had branches in London, Bruges, Barcelona, Valencia, Geneva, Avignon, Rome, Venice and Pisa and was connected to other companies that it practically controlled. Cosimo had also inherited by his father Giovanni or had acquired a large number of houses and trades in the town. He insisted with Eugene IV – using his money as a very convincing means – in having the Council of Ferrara of 1439, which established the union between the Latin and Greek churches moved to Florence. As a result, the town was invaded by throngs of petulant scholars from the East and clergymen, both miserable and eager for money, yet in possession of splendid pieces of ancient Greek culture. From then on, Greek tutors and codes eagerly headed to the palace in Via Larga. Fascinated by art and by ancient wisdom and a follower, perhaps not very competent yet enthusiastic, of Platonism that would become the main philosophy of the Florentine Renaissance, Cosimo profused his wealth and the profits originating from his businesses to encourage studies and to finance splendid works of art. In doing so, he never made the mistake of dissociating his name from Florence. From 1440 to 1464, the year of his death, his personal income had practically doubled, thanks to his ability and despite the very exorbitant expenses that only a superficial observer could have judged "useless". His hegemony over the town, exerted indirectly through families like the Pitti and the Soderini, was never opposed.

After miraculously saving Florence in the strife against the Visconti with the battle of Anghiari in 1440, Cosimo ruled prudently, even allowing or at least being unable to avoid the presence of some prior or political personality not exactly favourable to him. Yet, he promoted the establishment of new institutions like the Council of the Hundreds, founded in 1458 that was represented only by his most loyal supporters. In foreign matters, events forced him to almost "reverse his alliances". From the beginning of the fourteen century, Florence had always been loyal to Venice againsts Milan. The interests of the two states were complementary: the interests of Venice were maritime and prevalently oriented to the east, while those of Florence were territorial and oriented to the west. Over time the situation had changed. After acquiring Pisa and Livorno, Florence had gained access to the sea while on the other hand Venice, led by doge Foscari, had started a territorial expansion that worried the other Italian states. When a friend of Cosimo, Francesco Sforza, became the Duke of Milan, in 1454, the "reversal of alliances" was finally completed. From then on, Florence and Milan would have become allies to the detriment of Venice.

At the death of Cosimo in 1464, the power passed on to his son Piero, a very skilful businessman and politician with a rather unhealthy complexion (he was in fact known as "The Gouty"). A first attempt of some of the followers of Cosimo of taking advantage of his death to reverse or at least to limit the supremacy of the Medici through other noble families failed. Even after Piero's death, which occurred shortly after in 1469, the leadership of the Medici family, of the commercial company and of the state safely passed on to his two sons, Lorenzo and Giuliano. Both were young, but they had already been presented by their grandfather to the town as inheritors of the Medici family.

They also had different temperaments. Notwithstanding the apathy and sensual fascination of Giuliano, it was Lorenzo who reminded his fellow-citizens of Cosimo and was destined to become his direct successor, despite his scarcely handsome features that were counterpoised by a ready intelligence and a cynical political realism.

Lorenzo, "The Magnificent", has been widely praised, thanks mainly the favourable opinion of Gucciardini, who referred to him as the needle of the balance of Italian politics, thinking of him and of the very difficult political situation of the time. Lorenzo was a really great statesman and diplomat and always managed to mediate contrasting forces and avoid unbalances and significant contrasts. From several points of view he was not up to the role of his predecessor. He belonged to the "second generation" of statesmen; in other words he was born to govern. Although he often proved he had the necessary strength to maintain power, he never really appeared to be interested in public matters and in the art of governing, which had instead been the main characteristics of Cosimo. He was born – as they Byzantines said – in the "wealth", that is after his family had already consolidated its power and acted therefore as if he was entitled to everything. He didn't even share the attitude of his predecessor, who focused on living as a private citizen. Everything in him was inspired to the Augustean model of the *princeps*. He had a passion for chivalry games like tournaments and jousts and probably gave up the idea of giving a military tone to the family tradition because of his physical problems and the lack of military resources.

He has often been termed as a thorough supporter of letters and arts and a good patron. Even these considerations are rather exaggerated. It is true that he was a good poet and writer with an easy, fluid, prolific and sometimes pleasant style, but he preferred to let his friends and relatives spend their fortunes to sponsor important works of arts. His cousin,

Lorenzo di Pier Francesco, was the protector of Botticelli.

His friends Lucca Pitti, Francesco Sassetti, Giovanni Tornabuoni and Giovanni Rucellai commissioned work to Alberti and Ghirlandaio. In reality, Lorenzo used the extraordinary artistic talents of Florence as ambassadors. It was in this period and in the years that followed, that Florentine art expanded and exerted his supremacy over other Italian centres through the talents of Leonardo, Verrocchio, Botticelli and Pollaiolo, thus becoming the symbol of unachievable perfection and a model of renovation.

Lorenzo was not a good administrator. The branches of the Medici bank in London and Bruges declared bankruptcy in 1478 and the branch of Lyon almost followed the same fate in 1488. The long government of The Magnificent left the Medici company and the treasury of the Republic of Florence in a devastating situation.

He ruled over the subjected communities with great severity. In 1470 he repressed the rebellion of Prato, he subdued Volterra in 1472 because of the mines of allumen (before monopolising the mines of Tolfa). In 1478 he miraculously escaped a plot organised by the Pazzi and the Salviati, with the complicity of Pope Sixtus V and the King of Naples. It was on this occasion that Giuliano was killed. Noteworthy was the readiness with which Lorenzo prevented this event from becoming the pretext of a war that would have involved the whole of Italy. Because of the intelligence with which he managed to create an alliance with the Sforza in Milan and the Aragon family in Naples, aimed at limiting the expansion of the Pope and Venice, he was considered the saver of peace and the equilibrium of Italy. In the mean time however, he also prepared a series of constitutional instruments aimed at safeguarding his authority. In 1470 he created a restricted council that could control the Council of the Hundreds; in 1470 he organised a Council of the Seventies responsible for electing the Priors; in 1490 he again imposed his power by creating a Council of the Seventeen. All these organs were obviously under his direct control.

Lorenzo had however inherited from Cosimo the love for philosophy and the eagerness of discovering the primary principles of the world and of human life. The academy, founded on a platonic model, established in the villa of Careggi was to become the centre of philosophic and hermetic speculations and bring to light Marsilio Ficino. The centre also attracted Pico Pirandola, the great celebrator of human omnipotence and magic viewed as art of harmonising the life of humans and universe. An elevated and abstract view to which Angelo Poliziano and Sandro Botticelli would contribute both with their verses and with the forms and colours of a pictorial perfection that had never been attained before.

During the oligarchy of the Albizzi and the dictatorship of the Medici, the number of inhabitants and the size of Florence did not increase, although it had been significantly embellished with grandiose and beautiful works of art. In 1401 the Guild of Calimala had promoted a competition for the door of the baptistery, which had been won by Lorenzo Ghiberti who also sculptured, almost twenty-five years later, the large eastern door, called the "Door of Paradise". The differences between the two doors, which show respectively the characteristics of the Gothic and the fully mature Renaissance style that flourished twenty-five years later, is sufficient to illustrate the revolution of style, language, taste and technique. In 1418 the Wool Guild promoted a competition for the construction of the cathedral's dome. The contest was won by Filippo Brunelleschi, who completed his work by 1438, after solving difficulties of all kinds originating from the narrow-mindedness of the guilds, of many of his colleagues and of the governors. Yet the dome was built and stayed in its place for centuries, despite the forecasts of narrow-minded or envious spirits, representing the symbol of the town. "The surrounding hills are similar to the dome" was the expression used by Vasari to describe this work of art.

The season of Brunelleschi was the most important period and to a certain extent the final stage of the great public architecture of

Florence. We have used the term public, without making any distinction between laic and religious architecture, because works like the dome were both things mixed together. In about twenty years, the master designed, built or restructured several monuments like the portico of the Spedale degli Innocenti, the basilica of San Lorenzo, the church of Santo Spirito, the "rotonda" (round building) of the convent of Santa Maria degli Angioli and a part of the Palagio di Parte Guelfa. More or less in the same years – that is between the second and fifth decade of the century – the Guilds decorated the exterior of their Pantheon, Orsanmichele, with splendid statues representing their patron saints.

The town was also embellished thanks to the generous, although superb, contribution of the great families. Brunelleschi himself was forced to accept – and could not have behaved in any other way – the logic of the oligarchic power, when he built its patronage and self-glorification, when he built the Chapel of the Pazzi in Santa Croce, the Chapel of the Medici (the *Old Sacristy*) in San Lorenzo and Palazzo Pitti on the south bank of the river Arno at the feet of the hill of Boboli. Cosimo the Eldest commissioned Michelozzo the palace in Via Larga and the convent of San Marco. Giovanni Rucellai and Alberti were asked to build the palace and the loggia in Via della Vigna Nuova and the small church of San Pancrazio featuring a small chapel that resembled the configuration of the Holy Sepulchre of Jerusalem. The Strozzi asked Benedetto da Maiano and Simone del Pollaiolo to build their palace. The Florentines of the time – from the great artists down to the artisans of the most humble workshops – were skilled in all kinds of arts and techniques. They were expert in welding metals, making clocks and other mechanisms, in decorating embossed and gilded leather items and also in the art of printing, although they could never beat – by an hair's breadth – the glory of the Gütenberg. It is impossible to explain the passion of the scholars of the academy of astrology without taking into account the fact that Paolo dal Pozzo Toscanelli was busy in the same years studying Tolomeo and Strabone, questioning himself on the dimensions of the earth and installing the gnomon inside the dome of Brunelleschi to measure the position of the sun.

It was even a joyful and happy Florence. The Medici had encouraged the celebration of festivals, like Carnival and May Day, in addition to solemn public festivities like St. John at the end of June, during which the ruling class received a symbolic tribute in candles and banners from the subjected communities in the name of the patron saint and as a sign of loyalty. Lorenzo had transformed triumphal parades, tournaments and jousts into princely celebrations, during which the Medici boasted their full splendour.

Yet, if we look at it today, this flourishing season appears to be dimmed by a veil of sadness and anguish. Perhaps it is because of the beautiful *Stanzas* of Poliziano, which were never finished due to the sudden death of Giuliano; perhaps it is because of the portraits of Piero di Cosimo or the profiles engraved on medals, which almost look like funereal masks because of their immobility. "Creativity and imagination" were the key features of the Florentine artists and politicians of the 15th century, which were endlessly repeated from Rucellai down to Vasari. Two terms that perfectly describe a town that invented perspective, erected the dome of its cathedral without any inner frame and perhaps gave Christopher Columbus the inspiration to initiate his long journey.

Yet, this lost and always perfect age filters a geometric sadness. Perhaps, again, because of the smoke raising from the *bonfires of vanity* organised by Savonarola, in which most of these works were burnt; or because of the subsequent dispersion of creativity and imagination towards the Papal Rome or the courts of France; or even because of the last neurotic and shaded interpretations of the Renaissance style that degenerated in mannerism. Looking at the most beautiful artistic intuitions of Brunelleschi – the large concrete spans innervated by the grey *pietra serena* or by the brownish shade of *pietra forte* – it is inevitable to remember that the great master may have been inspired by the view of the lifeless walls that were used to cover the frescoes of churches to prevent devoted pilgrims from touching them and spreading the infection. From this age of plagues we have however inherited the availability of space destined to gardens, like, perhaps the harmony and clarity of the interiors designed by Brunelleschi. This is sometimes the evolution of art and history. Without the incredible ability of casting metals, we would have never had the "Perseus" of Benvenuto Cellini. Yet this ability had to be perfected over many decades, before the princes of Italy and Europe could use it for their statues and perhaps for their bells. And above all for their cannons.

Sons of Jove and of the rain of gold

Dying in 1492, Lorenzo had left the finances of the family and of the state in a devastating situation. In 1494 the Compagnia of the Medici could not avoid bankruptcy and in the mean time Piero, the son and successor of Lorenzo was disgracefully exiled from town, after being accused of lack of firmness in preventing the King of France, Charles VIII, from passing through Tuscany on his journey to Naples. For four years the town was torn apart by the strife between the followers of a Dominican friar with a prophetic spirit and with a great charisma, Girolamo Savonarola, and his opponents. Savonarola dreamt of Florence as a place finally purified from sin, of a "New Jerusalem", a republic under the reign ruled by Jesus Christ characterised by the union of civic virtues and Christian piety. At the same time, however, we was working to create a more "popular" regime. The main organ of the new government was the so-called Great Council, whose dimensions are evident from the size itself of the Room of the Five Hundred, inside the *Palazzo dei Priori*, which was specifically built for it. The most evident traits of the dictatorship of Savonarola are well-known and consisted in long penitentiary preaches, in bonfires of all the objects that represented luxury and in the raids of the squads of youths, who were actually animated by the fire of sacred hoodluminism. Savonarola had however the spirit of a great charismatic leader and a reasonable degree of political intuition. His attempt to "reform" the town – that is to give it new political institutions – was based on the example of Venice and on the balance between the aristocratic principles of the councils and the monarchic principles represented by the *doge*.

The followers of the Dominican friar, who fascinated artists like Sandro Botticelli or Pico della Mirandola, were called *piagnoni* (whiners) or *frateschi* (followers of the friars). They were opposed by the *arrabbiati* (angry ones), the supporters of an oligarchic republic based on Roman cultural and political models, and by the *palleschi* who fought for the return of the Medici.

The defeat of Savonarola originated from his conflict with the Pope. Excommunicated by Pope Alexander VI, the friar was unable to maintain his popularity that gradually faded, also as a consequence of the fact that most of the trade of Florence was seriously compromised by the wrath of the Pope and by the dispersion of the dominions of the town. The first alarming signal came from the rebellion of Pisa.

The death sentence of the friar, hanged on the stake in Piazza della Signoria in May 1498, did not solve the political difficulties the institutional crisis of Florence. The project inspired to the *doge* was finally put into practice in 1502 after the mediocre Pier Soderini was given the title of life gonfaloneer. The resuscitated republic survived rather honourably for ten years. It was at this time that Michelangelo sculptured the "David", the Christian symbol of a people fighting for freedom with the help of God. It was at this time that the guilds of the Rucellai, the Strozzi, the Gondi and the Guadagni experienced a new period of floridity.

Oligarchic and republic traits and influences of the republic of Savonarola lived together in this new experiment, which aimed at guaranteeing the ancient *libertas* of the town, but, as usual, was not ready to grant too much freedom to the underprivileged classes or to the subjected communities in the regional state. The men who celebrated Brutus and had adopted David as their symbol reacted very severely to the rebellion of

Pisa, which had managed – between 1494 and 1509 - to conquer and maintain its freedom.

Besides, this political experiment was in line with the European reality of the time, characterised by the war between France and Spain. The republican Florence supported, as it had traditionally done from the 13th century onwards, the French crown and managed to maintain its power perhaps thanks to its alliance. In 1512 a Spanish army invaded Tuscany and restored to power the successors of the Medici after disastrously sacking Prato. The town fell into the hands of the other son of Lorenzo, cardinal Giovanni, who was however elected Pope, with the name of Leo X, the following year. The Florentine signoria was then handed down to the third son of Lorenzo, Giuliano, Duke of Nemours. When he died in 1516, the only representative of the Medici Family was Lorenzo, Duke of Urbino, the son of Piero who had been exiled as a consequence of the events of 1494. Lorenzo died in 1518 and the government of the town was passed on to Alessandro, who was (at least officially) the son of Lorenzo of Urbino, and to cardinal Ippolito, the son of Giuliano of Nemours.

The real government, however, resided no longer in the *Palazzo dei Priori* that was occupied by a complaisant signoria, nor in Via Larga where the descendants of Cosimo still resided. The economic and political fortune of the Medici had again re-flourished, because the

Medici were now sitting in the sacred pontifical palaces, like Giovanni, the son of Lorenzo The Magnificent, who was elected Pope with the name of Leo X from 1513 to 1521, and Julius, the son of Giuliano, who had been stabbed to death in 1578 by the Pazzi family, elected with the name of Clemens VII who reigned from 1523 to 1534. The new eclipse of the Medici family partly originated from this pope, the real ruler of Florence after the death of Leo X. When the Pope signed an alliance with the French, adopting a political view opposed to Charles V, the latter occupied and sacked Rome with his troops in 1527, causing an insurrection to break out in Florence. Following a republic and Savonarola-like impetus, the population exiled once more the Medici family, because the Popes appeared to have committed more sinful actions than those that Girolamo had reproached to Alexander.

The gonfalonier Niccolò Capponi proclaimed Christ as the King of Florence, challenging the emperor. From then on, Florence would have had no more monarchs.

Charles V accepted the challenge. After signing a peace with the Pope during the Congress of Bologna in 1529, it was necessary to restore peace in Florence. Clemens expected a kind of refund from the emperor for the loss of the town, caused by the events of 1527. With incredible strength and passion, the population of Florence resisted for eleven months to the siege of the Emperor's and Pope's armies. It was Michelangelo himself who directed the works for the new fortifications. This time the Florentine David could do very little to fight the empire's Goliath. Defeated by famine and by the plague, stabbed in the back by a traitor, Florence surrendered.

The Pope had now understood that Florence had clearly demonstrated that the Medici family had to be anchored to something more solid than the continuous alternation of favours, violence, blackmails or the manipulation of the ruling organs and the "finances" of public offices. It was necessary to device something new that differed from the systems that the Medici had used, with varying ability and fortune, to rule over the town for over a century. In 1532, the Florentine state was transformed by the Emperor into a dukedom and Alexander, the son of Lorenzo of Urbino (although everyone actually believed he was the son of the Pope), was appointed as duke. After Alexander's murder, five years later, by a relative, Florence risked being reabsorbed by the empire, also because of the fact that after the death of Alexander there were no direct successors. Besides, the recognised leader of the Florentine republicans, Filippo Strozzi, was putting together an army to march on Florence from France, where he had been exiled. To save peace and avoid throwing the town once more in the vortex of conflicts between France and the empire, the Florentine magnates – among which there was also Gucciardini – elected a very young representative of a secondary branch of the Medici family, which descended from Lorenzo, the brother of Cosimo the Elder. The new duke was Cosimo, the eighteen year-old son of Giovanni "delle Bande Nere" – one of the few Medici with extraordinary military abilities – who had heroically died in 1527 fighting against the emperor's troops. A good star seemed to protect the young duke, who managed to defeat with his troops the army of the Strozzi in Montemurlo.

If we look at the Medici parabola with hindsight, the passage from the signoria to the principality – that occurred rather late in comparison with other Italian families – appeared to be fatally decreed. Cosimo I ruled with wisdom. He was aware of the fact that Florentines did not love him too much and this explains why he always focused on creating a Tuscan state, with an army that did not include any members of the ruling families (that were not given the opportunity of being armed) and with fortresses and palaces spread all over Tuscany. He became grand duke – a papal title rather than an imperial one – in 1569, after conquering Siena in 1555 and proclaiming himself duke of the town. The dukedoms of Florence and Siena were carefully separated and kept apart.

The advent of the Medici dukes and, later, of the grand dukes of the Hapsburg and Lorraine house coincides with a period marked by less significant historical events. Despite a very evident impoverishment – that followed somehow the destiny of the rest of Europe and was caused by the "revolution of prices" that affected the 16th century and the centuries that followed – some plagues, a few years of famine and several episodes of delinquency and corrupt customs, the town remained substantially loyal and disciplined under the government of princes, who managed, among other things, not to involve the town in further conflicts. Cosimo I supported the development of the port of Livorno, founded the Order of Santo Stefano to fight the Berber pirates, started reclaiming Valdichiana, Maremma and Valdinievole, also to sustain in some way the Florentine aristocracy, which was gradually becoming a class of landowners after the bankruptcy of several banks and the fall of trades. Despite this negative trend, the governments of Cosimo and those of his two sons, Francis I and Ferdinando I, experienced the same mercantile fortune of the Medici. Many workshops of the Silk Guild continued to survive.

The development of the town continued unaltered. Actually, the 16th century and the early years of the 17th century were dominated by three great architects: Giorgio Vasari, Bartolommeo Ammanati and Bernardo Buontalenti. Thanks to a system consisting in palaces, gardens, fortresses and galleries, the prince was able to pass from the city walls to the centre of the town without leaving his palace that housed the offices of his government. Ammannati transformed Palazzo Pitti into a ducal palace, where the court moved leaving the ancient palace that was named Vecchio (Old) after his move. From Palazzo Pitti, the duke could reach the Fortress of St. George or *Belvedere*, also built by Buontalenti, through the magnificent Boboli gardens. On the opposite side of the town stood the fortress of St. John or *Fortezza da Basso* (Lower Fortress).

In reality the two fortresses were never meant to oppose any enemy. They threatened the town with two cannons and were considered the keys of the capital of the dukedom. From the Belvedere the prince could pass through Palazzo Pitti, walk along a gallery built above *Ponte Vecchio* (the Old Bridge) and reach the Uffizi gallery built by the Vasari, which housed the state administrative office and, finally, the Old Palace.

Even the roads were affected by the change of regime. Via Maggio, which ran almost in parallel with Palazzo Pitti, tidily aligned the homes of the aristocratic families of the town and the bridge, built by Ammannati, joined it to the other bank of the river. The age to come, which has been sometimes been defined as the period of *vast enclosures* (orphanages, barracks, hospitals, prisons, ghettos) was getting closer. Buontalenti had in fact started reorganising, from 1570 onwards, the grid of unhealthy streets in the area between Santa Trinita, the Strozzi palace, the *Palazzo di Parte Guelfa* and the new market square. The area was destined to the ghetto where Jews were obliged to reside.

The passage from the republic to the principality was characterised by several problems, although the latter never totally cancelled the former. The number of statues in Piazza della Signoria gradually increased. The Judith of Donatello and the David of Michelangelo, the glories of a republic that was proud of its scarce forces yet strongly believed in God with an echoing the experience of the Republic of Savonarola, were soon flanked by the equestrian statue of Cosimo by Giambologna and by the fountain of Neptune, chosen by Ammannati to celebrate the founder of the Order of Santo Stefano, the new lord of the Tyrrhenian Sea. But the most imposing statue – after the Hercules by Bandinelli, representing the ancient symbol of the commune that had been acquired by the principality – was the Perseus of Cellini, who has been conveying ever since his austere and ironical message. Perseus raises his arm, with a gesture that resembles that of an headsman, the showing head of Medusa encircled by snails that symbolise the conflicts of the town. It was a clear admonition to the whole town, erected in the very same square where the population usually met. It is useful to remember that Perseus is a typical Medici hero. Just like the duke, Perseus, is the son of Jupiter and of the rain of gold that made Danae fertile and in which the god usually hid. Jupiter is the emperor, the prince of the dukedom. The rain of gold is the fortune of the Medici house.

As a result of the restructuring works of the Old Palace, which were made by Vasari and Battista del Tasso between 1540 and 1555 to adapt it to its new functions; of the loggia of the new market carried out by del Tasso; and of the noble palaces in Via Maggio, Florence acquired a mannerist look that integrated the previous ones. Even cultural institutions experienced a similar development.

The academic tradition, inaugurated in the Medici villa of Careggi, flourished and somehow compensated the lack of an institutional university. Cosimo was the promoter of the Florentine Academy and of the Academy of Fine Arts that were later followed by the foundation of the *Accademia della Crusca* and, in 1657, by the Galileian *Accademia del Cimento*.

Meanwhile even the traditions of Florentine music was preserved and developed thanks to the prestigious *Camerata de' Bardi*, established at the end of the 16th century.

The 17th century wasn't lucky for Florence either, despite the quality of dukes like Cosimo II and Ferdinando II, who granted his protection to Galileo. A flood of the river Arno, in 1589, was the cause of a long and very devastating famine. The production of wool and silk cloths drastically fell during the first half of the 17th century because of the reduction of the population originating from the plague that broke out between 1631-1633. The population later reached its original numbers and by the early years of the 18th century was once more around 70,000 inhabitants.

This decadence, highlighted by the poverty of an aristocracy of land owners in a region where land had always been rather poor, did not stop Florence from experiencing a reasonable flourishing Baroque period. Some examples of it can still be seen on the facade of Ognissanti by Matteo Nigetti, in the Teatine church of San Gaetano and of San Filippo Neri, both by Gherardo and Pier Francesco Silvani, and above all in the sumptuous church of Santissima Annunziata. Again a "Florentine" Baroque, measured and faithful to classic traditions, yet characterised by extravagant inventions. Creativity and imagination, as usual.

The age of the Lorraine family

The atmosphere of Florence, between the 17th and 18th centuries, was not so dull. The ruling class naturally hung on to its estates managed with the *métayage* system. The protectionism of Colbert in France had drastically reduced the production of wool and silk of the Florentine workshops. Thus, Florence pullulated with miserable and starving beggars, who contributed to the growth of famine, vice, misery and corrupt customs. But there were also those who managed to make a fortune, like the Capponi and the Corsini, who exploited the fortune of Popes like the Florentine Urbanus VIII, or like Lorenzo Corsino, who would have later become Clemens XII. Large palaces that resembled the Roman and Papal ones, were erected to celebrate the wealth of the families who owed their fortune to the Papacy. The Corsini palace was started by Pier Francesco Silvani and completed by Ferri, while Capponi palace was built by Ruggeri. Meanwhile even another family, the Riccardi, became so wealthy to purchase the old Medici palace in Via Larga, built by Michelozzo, and have it enlarged and decorated by Luca Giordano. Religious building activities also flourished. Ruggeri completed the church of San Firenze and Ferri embellished the south bank of the river Arno adding a small little dome to the church of Cestello. Culture did not languish either, because Florence was the place of abode of doctors like Redi and Cocchi and of erudite scholars like Magliabechi, Magalotti and Lami. Included in the grand tours of noble families, Florence became a compulsory stop, a temple of art, perhaps very silent and a bit degraded, yet sill dignified and closely connected with the rest of Europe. It is worth remembering the sumptuousness of the *Società Colombaria* and of the Botanical Society, which were both established in the first half of the 18th century and the importance acquired by the porcelain manufacturing plant of Doccia, founded in 1737 by Marquis Ginori.

The Medici family faded away among corrupt customs and bigot sadness. Ferdinando II and his son Cosimo II were unable to control their homosexual tendencies within the limits of dignity, conditioned perhaps by unlucky marriages. Gian Gastone, the son of Cosimo, added to this kind of family vice a sort of pathological and fatalistic indolence. But these were times in which diplomacy - with wigs, dentelles and even armies - decided the fate of people and of states in chancellor's offices. Gian Gastone hadno successors and at any rate the fate of Tuscany had already been decided in 1734 - three years before his death - by the two great powers that the last Medici had struggled against, that is France and Austria.

Some scholars of law thought it was possible to restore the Republic, but there were only whims. Although many members of the Tuscan aristocracy would have preferred a successor of the Bourbon family, France played another card. The dukedom of Tuscany was handed over to Stanislaw Leczyinski, the father-in-law of Luis XV and former king of Poland. Francis Stephen, the husband of the Empress Maria Theresa of Hapsburg was compensated for his loss with Tuscany. The French crown clearly preferred a satellite state in the centre of Europe, that is the wealthy and densely populated Lorraine, to a dukedom in the centre of Italy, which was certainly rich with historical monuments yet very impoverished. Besides, the house of Lorraine owed "rights" over Tuscany that dated back to the 12th century and originated from their union with the Canossa family. This way, Tuscany that had traditionally belonged to the empire faced the risk of becoming one of the many possessions of the House of Hapsburg, like at the time of the death of Alexander. Even on this occasion, the situation was solved by the magnates of Florence. It was in fact decided that after the death of Stefano Francesco the imperial and Tuscan crown would not be joined. The empire would have been handed over to the first son of the House of Hapsburg, while Tuscany was to be passed on to his second son.

The mediocre arc of triumph of Jean N. Jadot, facing the door of San Gallo, is the only architectural memory of the twenty-eight years of this reign, which lasted from 1737 to 1765. Francis Stephen never resided in the town and Florentine did not appear to claim his presence. Actually, an inquisition trial organised against a member of the Masonry loggia, established a few years earlier in Florence by some Englishmen (the first, practical sign of the love of Florence for England equalled only by the equivalent feelings English people showed for Florence), was considered almost an insult to the prince, who belonged himself to the Masonry. The latter had already been condemned by Pope Clemens 12th, a member of the Corsini family, one of the most powerful and noble families of the time who had openly showed their disappointment for the defeat experienced by the Bourbon candidate as successor of the Medici. The scandal almost looked like a kind of nasty trick.

Although the relations with the distant and disinterested Francis Stephen were never very warm, the music changed when his second son, Leopold, became Grand Duke of Tuscany in 1865. Leopold ruled Tuscany for over twenty-five years, when the death of his brother Joseph II obliged him to return to Vienna to become Holy Roman Emperor himself.

Florentines immediately realised, upon his arrival, that Leopold was a capable ruler, who could be in some way considered a typical representative of the enlighted despotism of his age. When he arrived, Florence was on its knees due to a severe famine.

The new Grand Duke, determined to solve the problem and a follower of physiocratic philosophies, lucidly and rationally applied free-trade notions to agriculture and eliminated all the ancient duties and privileges – especially ecclesiastic – that prevented or even hindered the exchange of real estate. The *Accademia dei Georgofili* is still today a very valuable example of his emphasis on renovation. Even the old guilds were somehow suppressed; Leopold hoped in fact that this would stimulate manufacturing and commercial activities. An intense policy of reforms, institutional and judicial rationalisation – to the disadvantage also of ecclesiastic privileges – and of reclaiming operations soon brought to new life Florence and the whole grand dukedom. These activities were actually completed by the project for a new Constitution, which was never implemented.

His reform that decentralised the administration of the single towns to local and independent municipal administrations, from 1784 onwards, was a great success. The Grand duke clearly showed he intended abandoning the old tradition according to which towns were represented by oligarchies that passed their offices down to their inheritors. 1774 was therefore the year of birth of the modern municipal administration of Florence.

Many have believed that the climate of these years – undoubtedly with sound reasons – stimulated the growth and development of the catholic-liberal thought or liberal-democratic thought, which would have inaugurated a tradition for the ruling and intellectual classes of the town. The Bishop Scipione dei Ricci, who was known to support Giansenism with the protection of the court, devoted himself for some years to the renovation of the Tuscan church. Others, like Filippo Mazzei or Giovanni Fabbroni, with their passion for the American revolution, anticipated the political ideas of a future "left" wing that would have had a long and articulated history in Florence. We should not really be surprised to discover that Giovanni Fantoni and Filippo Buonarroti lived in the Florence of Leopold.

The death of Emperor Joseph II, in 1790, transferred the empire to his brother, the Grand duke of Tuscany. Leopold left the town to his second son, Ferdinando III, who was barely twenty years old at the time he became Grand duke. He was also a good ruler. But the fate of Europe was really being decided in Paris. The Revolution reached Florence first in the shape of a counter-reactionary movement – although insurrections like the *Viva Maria* were more of a reaction to the reforms of Leopold rather than to the news that came from France – and later with the usual confusion of French armies fighting against Austrian and Russian armies.

Napoleon finally managed to win the game in Tuscany, that is in a region that had given birth to his ancestors. In 1801, Florence became the capital of the Reign of Etruria under Ludovico I of Bourbon-Parma.

The new state existed only on the maps. It lived only until 1807, when it fell leaving behind a long period of constitutional uncertainty. Between 1808 and 1809, the region was directly annexed to the French Empire and again transformed into a grand dukedom between 1809 and 1814 and assigned to one of the sisters of the emperor, Elisa Baciocchi. For several months in 1814, Florence even experienced the occupation of the troops of Gioacchino Murat. The Grand duke Ferdinando managed – finally – to return in April 1815. After his death, the grand dukedom was passed on to this son Leopold I, also known with the nickname of Canapone, who would have reigned until 1859.

Despite the dramatic events of these years, it is worth noticing that the Florentine reasonability, and to some extent laziness and scepticism, prevented almost always the political situation from becoming too extreme and unbearable.

Florence had the Alberti fighting for freedom, but never had real Jacobins. It experienced the *Viva Maria* insurrections, but never really witnessed strong extremist passions. Using the comparison of the colours universally celebrated by Stendhal, we can say that the Florentine red rather resembled a pink and that the black looked more like a grey.

This is clearly reflected by the traits of one of the Carnival masks of the town, *Stenterello*, who is always starving and scared, caustic and slightly cynical, but yet reflects the satirical attitude of the town with less passion than *Pasquino* and less tragicalness than *Pulcinella*. Just like the Jacobin and later Napoleonic Liberté had never really been despotic, the Hapsburg *Return of Astrea* was never really repressive. Actually the tone of the power of Ferdinando and later of his son Leopold was rather sleep-inducing, careful in rounding off sharp edges and as general rule rather good-natured. Even those years coincided with a period of good government and of industriouspublic works.

Meanwhile, Florence was increasingly becoming, for different reasons that not were not foreign to one another nor opposed – artistic and cultural on the one hand and political on the other – the Mecca of travellers and foreign residents. Despite the dislike of Giacomo Leopardi, the town was very much loved by all those who were fascinated by the love tributed to the town of the river Arno by Vittorio Alfieri and Ugo Foscolo. It was Foscolo who actually eternally celebrated the town as a symbol of beauty and temple of the glories of Italy with his "Sepolcri". Later, Alessandro Manzoni transformed the high-class Florentine dialect into the language of all Italians, thus finally legitimating the myth of the *Risorgimento* and of the nation that considered the role of the Florentine history a necessary element of the identity of a new united homeland.

It is symptomatic – or we could define prophetical now that so much emphasis is placed on the importance of the union of Europe – to notice that many foreigners contributed to the discovery of this identity. This is the case of Jean Charles Léonard Simonde (the so-called "Sismondi") who celebrated the Commune of the Middle Ages as a paradigm of freedom. Or the case of his fellow countryman Jean Pierre Vieusseux, the founder of the *Gabinetto Viesseux* and of the magazine *The Anthology* that grouped the most modern Florentine intellectuals of the nobles families of the town. All of them agreed – including Capponi, Ridolfi and Ricasoli – that cultural and political renovation needed to necessarily be pursued with consideration and moderation.

The grand ducal government followed these ferments very carefully without showing too much approval nor condemning them. Florence and Tuscany were an island of moderation in a severe climate inaugurated by the Congress of Vienna. The most liberal representatives of the Florentine *intellighentia*, on the other hand, never fully adhered to more democratic ideas, unlike the intellectuals in Livorno. Probably this was also due to the fact that they strongly believed that Leopold II would have soon or later re-established the constitutional monarchy of this predecessor.

The years between 1848 and 1849 demolished most of these illusions and deteriorated the idyll between the Grand duke – who lived in exile in Gaeta since January 1849, though he had granted his citizens the Statute a year earlier and returned to his throne thanks to the rather useless support of the Austrian military force – and the Florentine cultural and political elites. Public opinion split into two factions. On the one hand there were the so-called supporters of autonomy, who were not ready to give up to the independence of Tuscany, and the annexationists, like Baron Ricasoli, on the other hand, who were firmly convinced that it was necessary to annex Tuscany to the monarchy of the

Savoia. More openly democratic and republic tendencies were favourably welcomed only by a consistent fringe of the middle and middle-low classes and especially by the craftsmen. This explains why the crisis of 1859-60 was solved rather easily, although even on this occasion the protagonist of the events – Bettino Ricasoli – did not back out despite being intimidated.

The grand duke peacefully accepted to be exiled; the illusions of creating a monarchy that could be "independent" under the guide of a member of the Bourbons or a successor of Napoleon (the Prince Gerolamo Bonaparte), which would have obviously pleased the French Emperor, were abandoned and a plebiscite – that took place in a rather troublesome yet never cocrcive atmosphere as elsewhere – voted the annexation of Tuscany to the constitutional monarchy of the Savoia. The protocols of the armistice of Villafranca had actually established that Tuscany should have been returned to the Lorraine family. But events overwhelmed the agreements. The decisions taken by the noble and high bourgeoisie classes that supported annexionism --at the time these decisions were taken – did not draw fine distinctions. It is true they believed in freedom, yet they were not ready to sacrifice their plans to the benefit of the plans of others.

The government of the Hapsburg – Lorraine family had lasted over a century and had left its discrete imprint even in the layout and architecture of Florence. The French domination instead had left very little behind. The Lorraine had promoted the foundation of the Museum of Physics and Natural History, known as "La Specola", the gallery of the Accademia and the restructuring – with a slight rococo touch – of the church of Carmine, which had been destroyed by a fire in 1711. The real artistic genius of the age of Leopold was Gaspare Maria Paoletti, the court architect, who had enlarged the section of Palazzo Pitti facing the Boboli gardens (the famous "Palazzina della Meridiana"), a part of the Villa of Poggio Imperiale and the jewel of the White Hall of Palazzo Pitti, which could only suit a town like Florence (and Vienna). Even court architecture had maintained a kind of sober style. Understandably enough, since the grand dukes of the Hapsburg family clearly emphasised their austerity with the palace of Schonbrunn. The work of Paoletti was later continued by Cacialli, another court architect.

The passage from the neo-classic to the romantic style – and therefore to the new gothic style - was somehow supported and managed by another very skilful architect, Gaetano Baccani, who offered with the Palazzo Borghese built in Via Ghibellina – with a slight delay – a wide-ranging Napoleonic setting (a less suffocating empire style). Over the same years, he built the Neo-gothic turret in the Torrigiani gardens, between San Frediano and Porta Romana, and at the beginning of the forties of the 19th century he erected the bell tower of Santa Croce. In the mean time, the architect Niccolò Mattias had started building the New-gothic facade of the large Franciscan church, that is a remarkable example of a balanced use of polychrome marbles.

Despite the many projects, the facade of very few churches had been completed. San Lorenzo and the church of Carmine were still without a facade and that was probably their fortune. The original facade of the cathedral had been demolished in 1587 to be replaced by a new one that was never completed. It was only in 1871 that Emanuele De Fabris started to rebuild it, although the works themselves continued until 1887. A monument to romantic historicism and to the same celebrative rhetoric that inspired paintings like "La Cacciata del duca d'Atene" by Stefano Ussi.

The three-colour marbles of the cathedral's facade (the original green and white marblehad been integrated with the red symbolising patriotism) date back to when Florence became the capital of Italy and to the general atmosphere of this period. The same that brought about the demolition of the city walls and the organisation of large boulevards, the building of Piazzale Michelangelo and the central area that once corresponded to the Old Market, known today as Piazza della Repubblica, which resumed its original splendour after years of decadence. In other words, the work of Giuseppe Poggi.

When Florence became the capital of Italy, the first railway station that had been built outside the city walls in 1847 had already been replaced – in the following year – by the station of Santa Maria Antonia, behind the church of Santa Maria Novella. In 1851, a convention signed by the railway companies of the Papacy, the Grand dukedom of Tuscany, the dukedoms of Parma and Modena and the Austrian Empire had almost led to the creation of a connection between Rome, Lombardia and Veneto. Perhaps this fact was meant to anticipate the idea of a federal Italy rather than a united one, which respected traditions yet acknowledged the rights of legitimate sovereigns and did not seem to support the nationalistic passion that would have devoured Europe over the decades to come. Things worked out differently.

Florence, that became capital of Italy between 1865 and 1870 – a period characterised by statesmen, entrepreneurs, demolitions, town planning activities (that had undoubtedly deprived the historical centre of his original nature, but had also eliminated several decaying buildings) and a dynamism increasingly influenced by foreigners – fully represented the dynamism that symbolised Italy after its union that was imposed by the conservatory parties. Yet in Florence many traits seemed to live together peacefully. The welcoming yet ironically reserved attitude, a rational view that occasionally opened to esotericism, inherited by the Renaissance and passed over through the age of Leopold; lived together with a "cultured" attitude that experienced very flourishing periods but was unable to avoid the decadence originating from very narrow horizons (although the situation was occasionally enlivened by more than one genius), influenced by several forms of moderate, laic, moderate and radical forms of narrow-minded attitudes; and with the passionate and sometimes rude attitude of Soffici and Pratolini, who were however far from rude themselves.

A provincialism that was encouraged by the sensation of being the centre of the world. Perhaps the counterpart of a love for foreigners that is unable to escape the risks of cultural colonisation? Perhaps it is really so. The fact is that Florentines don't seem to have realised that the age in which debates broke out for the doors of the Baptistery and for the Brunelleschi models of the cathedral's dome have gone for ever and cannot be brought back by the luxury of the Pitti Men fashion parades and the prestigious shops of Via Tornabuoni. The age of tails and wigs during which Austrian princesses refused to reside in town have long gone by. And gone for ever is also the age iof villas with New-medieval furniture that were greatly admired by foreigner lovers between the two centuries and between the two wars (and by Gabriele D'Annunzio himself). Florence hardly realises that for a long time it has almost been considered the outskirts quarter of Vienna, of London and Paris. Yet this never could be said of Turin or Milan either. Although it risks looking more like the outskirts of New York, it will never look like - even in the worst of cases - a peripheral district of Milan. Despite its degradation, its provincialism, its commercialisation and the invasion of tourists - even despite Florentines? - Florence is always the same. A glory of the world. Yet if it continues to be so in future, this will only be thanks to its past. *Rien que l'histoire.*

THE SMALL PACINI COLLECTION

1. Breve Storia di Pisa (new edition)
   Ottavio Banti
   English edition: A short history of Pisa
   German edition: Kurze geschichte von Pisa
   Spanish edition: Breve historia de Pisa

2. Breve Storia di Firenze
   Franco Cardini
   English edition: A short history of Florence
   German edition: Kurze geschichte der stadt Florenz
   Spanish edition: Breve historia de Florencia

3. Come far cadere la Torre di Pisa (new edition)
   Piero Pierotti

4. Breve storia di Venezia
   Gherardo Ortalli, Giovanni Scarabello
   English edition: A short history of Venice
   German edition: Kurze geschichte Venedigs

5. Breve storia dell'Isola d'Elba
   Anna Benvenuti Papi
   German edition: Kurze geschichte der Insel Elba

6. Le città italiane dell'età di Dante
   Giovanni Cherubini

7. Breve Storia di Siena
   Giuliano Catoni
   English edition: A short history of Siena

8. Breve Storia di Lucca
   Paolo Bottari
   German edition: Kurze geschichte von Lucca

9. *Breve storia della Torre di Pisa*
   Piero Pierotti
   English edition: A short history of the Tower of Pisa

10. Breve storia di Prato
    Franco Cardini

11. Breve storia di Pistoia
    Alberto Cipriani
    English edition: A brief history of Pistoia

12. Breve Storia di Viareggio
    Tommaso Fanfani

13. Breve Storia di Livorno
    Olimpia Vaccari
    Lucia Frattarelli Fischer
    Carlo Mangio
    Giangiacomo Panessa
    Maurizio Bettini

Printed in March 2006
by Industrie Grafiche Pacini Editore S.p.A.
Via A. Gherardesca • 56121 Ospedaletto • Pisa
Telephone 050 313011 • Telefax 050 3130300
Internet: http://www.pacinieditore.it